MOONLIT KISS

A VENICE ROMANCE

AMY MCKINLEY

ARROWSCOPE PRESS, LLC

Moonlit Kiss (A Venice Romance)

Copyright © 2021 Amy McKinley

An abridged version of Moonlit Kiss was previously published in With Love From Venice (Voyages of the Heart anthology).

(p) **ISBN-13**: 978-1-951919-08-5

(e) **ISBN-13**: 978-1-951919-07-8

Publisher Arrowscope Press, LLC; www.arrowscopepress.com

Editing— Kate Birdsall, Line Editor, Taylor Anhalt, Proofreader, Red Adept Editing

Cover Design—T.E. Black Designs; www.teblackdesigns.com

Author photo provided by—Brookelyn Anhalt of lovely.life.photography; https://www.facebook.com/LovelyLifePhotography-102253596490708

Interior Formatting & Design— Arrowscope Press, LLC; www.arrowscopepress.com

Stepping off the plane at Marco Polo Airport felt like a homecoming so real, so undeniable, that my throat clenched, a mist of tears coated my eyes, and I clutched the arm of a stranger. I'd been there before—just not in this lifetime.

I'd often heard tales of one's psyche recognizing places, ties from the past, even soul mates. And to me, Venice, Italy, was home.

After all, Mom was from Tuscany. Why Venice felt so familiar was perplexing, but it was surely due to our family's history in Italy. Mom had immigrated to America with her family when she was young. I'd grown up on Italian food and stories from both my grandparents. I spoke the language fluently and longed to someday visit my ancestral homeland in the rural hills of Tuscany. When I met Francesca, who hired me to restore a fresco painting in Venice, and since Mom's cancer was in remission, it was an opportunity I couldn't pass up.

After leaving the airport, I should have found the villa I would be staying at rent free to unpack and get a good night's sleep. That wasn't happening. Wired from the long flight, I decided to experience the floating city under the moonlight. From what I'd read, the winding streets of Venice were safe for a woman at night, so I had no worries. Besides, it was dark, and Francesca Marcello's mural would have to wait a few hours until daylight anyway.

I was glad it was the fall, the perfect time to visit Venice with its cooler temperatures and the tourist season ending. After a change of footwear then sharing a water taxi, I strolled through the winding streets, my rolling suitcase bumping along behind me, toward Piazza San Marco, or Saint Mark's Square. The heavy perfume of fall flowers mixed with the salt from the nearby water coated the air. The sky darkened, and the moon cast its rays on age-old buildings steeped in history. My pace slowed to take in the unique gothic architecture, studying its classic beauty.

For once, I didn't worry about losing my way. Under the amber glow of streetlamps, minutes dripped by while I feasted my eyes on fresco—or *affresco*—aka painting into lime plaster, done in brilliant contours. My rubber-boot-clad feet led the way, and I came upon the piazza as if I'd strolled the same path hundreds of times.

Not once had I needed to refer to the map I'd pulled up on my phone. It was as if I'd been there before and walked those streets hundreds of times already. Maybe I had but in another lifetime. *How else can I explain my intimate knowledge of the winding streets of Venice when I'd never stepped foot on the floating city?*

Enticing notes of music lured me around a corner to an orchestra stand in front of a *ristorante*. Bright lights reflected in the partially flooded square. My heart kicked up a notch, and my soul sighed as strains of Vivaldi's renowned summer concerto neared the thunderous pitch of "The Storm" and urged me to stay awhile.

Tourists and locals wandered the outer edges of the square on the passerelle, walkways elevated above the water, and their reflections shimmered in the rippling surface that filled the inner portion of the piazza. The flooding from the Adriatic Sea lagoon was minimal. I soaked up the sights around me, giddy that I was standing amidst such history. My gaze darted from one iconic building to the next. The Basilica San Marco church dominated the east side of the square, flanked by the Campanile di San Marco bell tower.

I ordered wine and *cicchetti*, Venetian tapas-style finger food, then found a seat farthest from the rising water. Inviting laughter and companionable conversation floated around me as I sipped my wine. The bell tolled nine o'clock. Easing back in my chair, I watched people and snacked as the concerto transitioned to autumn then winter with dramatic and emotional tempo shifts.

My pulse pounded in time with the violin strains as excitement overwhelmed my senses—*this is where I'm meant to be*. I'd snatched up the offer to work in Venice without a second thought, as the floating city was a place I'd planned to visit someday. Since I was there, I couldn't imagine leaving when the painting was completed.

There was something so magical about the place. My mealtime in the square passed much too quickly. Ten o'clock neared. I'd promised Francesca, whom I'd instantly liked when she'd first contacted me about the job, a phone call when I arrived. She was in her early seventies, and I worried the hour was too late. *Better do that now.*

A cool breeze from the lagoon sent goose bumps dancing along my skin, and I tugged my light cardigan close around my body, warding off the early October chill. Digging through my backpack, I found my cell then scrolled through the contacts to locate Francesca's number. I pressed the button to connect the call then waited. It rang twice before she picked up. I filled her in, sharing that I had arrived and had stopped for a bite to eat.

"I'm so glad you got there safely, Gianna."

"The flight was uneventful, which is what I'd hoped for. How is your vacation so far?" She wasn't there to greet me because she was traveling with several close friends.

"It is wonderful." She sighed. "We arrived in France tonight and then are off to Spain then Portugal. I hope you'll be all right alone in the villa?"

"Of course." The final strains of Vivaldi's winter concerto heralded the end of the orchestra's entertainment. I chose not to stay until the bell tolled at midnight, when the city would begin to shut down. I stifled a yawn then stood and slung my backpack over my shoulder, my phone pressed to my ear. "I'm looking forward to working on the mural at first light."

"Oh no. Not tomorrow." Her voice was warbled. "I've arranged for you to take a gondola ride to soak in the atmosphere of Venice during the daytime. Think of it as creative inspiration."

I attempted to decline, but Francesca wouldn't take no for an answer. Before we hung up, I agreed to her generous offer. Beneath the glow of the streetlamps, I turned the corner, dragging my luggage through hidden alleys and bridges passing over small inlets. One by one, shadows cast by each gas lamp led me through a dark labyrinth—no map could have guided me so well.

I would be staying in Francesca's villa for the next few months, working a dream job that I couldn't believe I'd landed. Francesca was a supporter of a nonprofit dedicated to preserving Venice's artistic heritage. While I wasn't a member of that particular organization, she'd sought me out after seeing several of my restoration projects and my own artwork.

I shivered. The night was changing—warm air mixed with the dropping evening temperatures, ushering in tendrils of fog that wafted in long strips along the canal, like eerie fingers seeking something that evaded their grasp. Adjusting my backpack, I again tugged my cardigan tightly around my body and quickened my pace, the map featured on my phone shoved back in my pocket.

The villa was a few blocks away and across the canal. A sense of déjà vu nipped at me as I made my way down the meandering streets, which I didn't seem to need my map for. *How is this familiar? There will be a bridge not too far ahead, where I will cross. On the other side will be the Marcello home.* I was to have the first of four floors to myself, and Francesca said no one else would be in residence for a couple of weeks. A wave of fatigue swept over me as I walked through tufts of mist. It was late, and I wanted to find my room.

The fog thickened, and icy awareness tiptoed along my spine, feeling a sense of familiarity as I passed the stretch of cafés and shops. The old-world charm of the buildings played an enticing game of peekaboo through the haze. I wanted to stop and study their exquisite designs before I lost sight of them altogether.

It was after ten, and a hush had descended over the city of canals, and I felt history's presence acutely. I rubbed my arms as I frowned at the eerie, heavy clouds affected my sense of well-being. My ears played tricks on me, and I swore the deep timbre of a man's voice echoed through the dense air. I tried to shake the unease that scratched along my skin. I must have been having an auditory hallucination—maybe it was a weird trick of the fog.

Time stilled as a cloudlike mass tumbled through the streets, distorting my sense of direction. An anguished cry echoed around me. I stumbled before catching myself, the feeling of déjà vu so strong that I questioned my reality.

"Sophia!"

I gasped. His deep baritone made it feel like a vise circled my heart. I paused as chills erupted over my body. *I know that voice.* Anguish dripped from his voice, and my feet remained rooted in place.

His desperate bellow spurred me to action, and I raced blindly through the dense haze, running to him instead of away.

My footsteps thudded on the pavement, my luggage careening precariously behind me. A minute passed then another. He continued to shout, the tormented sound echoing along the canal and bouncing off the residences that flanked it. A flash of light danced across the water's lapping surface. I skidded to a halt, mere steps from plummeting in.

A scuffle sounded to my left, and I turned. There, not more than a foot away, the fog parted to reveal an imposing man, perhaps a few years senior to my twenty-five, dressed in black trousers and a worried white button-down shirt.

His haunting gray gaze collided with mine. My heart swelled, its tempo increasing to alarming rates. And I drowned in my own pain, gasping through my intense agony.

Even if only in a dream, I'd seen him before and hadn't needed to look to recognize those gray eyes, how they'd once unnerved me, and how they still could. Wavy dark-mahogany hair that tended to defy all attempts to tame it brushed the edges of his collar. My fingers curled, and a desire to touch the soft strands beat in my chest.

How I knew him, I didn't fully understand. Nothing made sense, not my reactions or my actions since I'd set foot in the floating city. Tears rolled unchecked down my face, and my eyelids drifted shut. Time stood still. It was impossible, but… I knew the man, somehow. Tremors shook my hands until I clasped them together.

I sensed his approach. My body responded—it always had and always would. I felt a cool, featherlight touch on my face as he swept back a few strands that had fallen from my messy bun, as if he'd done it a thousand times before. My lips tingled as his brushed across mine in the lightest of caresses.

The spicy tang of leather and whiskey teased my awareness, and I opened my eyes. *What am I doing—allowing?* The deep sense of longing continued to suffocate me. I dropped my gaze to his lips and swayed. *Forbidden.* I wanted to bargain with him, with fate. One taste was all I wanted. *He's not real.*

"I've missed you." His husky voice wrapped me in a drugging desire. "Every night, I've searched for you, Sophia."

With a deep inhalation, I forced myself to face what I feared wasn't really there. Tilting my head to meet his gaze, I felt an icy chill on my cheek before his hand fell away. I blinked up at the stunning man towering over me. Arresting, chiseled features complemented a well-built frame that looked as if he could carry the weight of the world. It was an illusion. Neither of us could.

I'd dreamed of him, but I hadn't imagined him to be real. "I'm not—"

"Shh, my love." His eyes misted. "It's my fault. All of it."

I had to get away from the madness. *Maybe it's the wine.* I tore my gaze from him and looked around. The fog coated everything in each direction—I could only see a foot in front of me on all sides.

I was impossibly turned around *but not alone.*

Seconds ticked by as we stood before one another. I had no choice. "I'm afraid I'm lost."

A sad smile curved his lips. "As I've been, my sweet." He moved to stand beside me. "Come. I'll walk you home." A fierce frown marred his face, and I took a step back. "But not there… not to *him.*"

Him who? No one was supposed to be in the house. "I'm staying across the river, at the Marcello home."

A dazzling smile curved his kissable lips, and my body melted—the moment of wariness fled. "That's where I'd planned to take you."

I was a fool to do it, but I walked with him anyway. We fell into a companionable silence, our shoes scuffing along the cobbled stones. By his side, I felt safe. I wanted to learn more about him. The streets of Venice weren't known to be dangerous, and I didn't have a lot to lose.

The haze that encased the island had somehow soaked into my brain. I shook my head, trying to rid my mind of the hold the man seemed to have over me. "Who are you?"

He paused and turned to look at me. I mirrored his movements. Alarm briefly lit his eyes until sadness darkened them from gray to obsidian. "Giovanni. I am yours, Sophia, and you are mine. I've waited so long… now that you are here, I must confess my deep regret for putting you at risk for a foolish day by the shore."

This has gone on long enough. While I wanted to cling to every word he said, I was an imposter to his memory, his damaged mind. He needed to know. My conscience couldn't carry the weight of leading him on. Something was wrong, and I didn't want to contribute to his pain. "I'm sorry, Giovanni, for whatever happened to Sophia." My fingers stretched out to touch him before I thought better of it. "But I'm not her."

He gestured for us to continue down the walkway. "I will forever envision you in the arms of the gods," he purred sensually, as if I hadn't spoken to deny his delusion. A frown pulled at his lips. "Perhaps if we'd tossed them a coin, they would have watched over us, and we would have encountered only tame waters."

I couldn't follow his riddles and chose to let them roll off me. We turned. Nausea punched me in the gut as we traveled between two houses and stepped onto a bridge that spanned the distance over the canal. The swift jolt of sickness left me as soon as we arrived on the other side. *Weird.* The entire encounter had been odd. He paused, and I followed his gaze.

My breath caught from the impact of the astonishing fresco painting, and I hungrily devoured the moonlit sight before me. *The mural.* I was intimately acquainted with it, as I had been commissioned to work on it. Giovanni's voice jolted me back to the fact that I wasn't alone.

"My second-greatest regret is that it wasn't finished in time, and as such, I could not leave."

CHAPTER 2

After parting with Giovanni the night before, I'd gone inside the Marcello residence and crawled into bed with his parting words swirling in my overtaxed mind. Beneath a fluffy duvet, exhaustion lured me into a deep sleep until it was time to wake for Francesca's prearranged tour, which would commence in an hour. I had enough time to grab coffee and get a plan going for what supplies I needed for the restoration work I was hired to do.

Wanting to view the mural in the daylight, I hastily prepared a cup of coffee then stepped outside. Light played over the surface of the mural on the outer wall of the Marcello home. The warm rays enhanced the romanticism of the fresco before me, lovingly revealing how the former artist's bold use of color and gifted hand tied together the masterpiece. It took my breath away. Something about the work spoke to me in ways I couldn't put to words, and I blinked past a mist of tears. Seeing the mural in the daylight instead of by the light of the moon made a lasting impression in my psyche. Both had called to me, but the sunlight pulled me into the scenes of a man and woman deeply in love, depicted in every nuance of their postures. It rang a chord in my body that I could not identify.

With a small step back, I skimmed the painting again. The outer building's wall had a panel of vine-covered arches, each showcasing a different scene. The mural consisted of a total of three panels. The first showed the back of a man and woman as they walked hand in hand across a canal by bridge. The second was of the same couple enjoying a gondola ride, their faces in profile only. The third was unfinished. I bent to inspect the bottom portion of the panel, my knees cracking as I did. The fresco had fared remarkably well over the years. It would still have to be cleaned before I could repair the softly peeling Venetian plaster. Soon, the fresco would look brand-new, though it was clearly over a century old. I straightened then skimmed over the rest of the panels. The couple wore the clothing of the era. Their faces were obscured in the scenes, but their intense romance was transmitted with hypnotizing precision.

I was surprised by its excellent condition as I briefly assessed the work I would have to do. I feared Francesca was paying me more than I normally would have charged, especially with the free accommodations. I would have to rectify that as well. Taking advantage of an elderly woman did not sit right with me.

My gaze locked on the blank third panel, and Giovanni's comment about the unfinished mural being one of his greatest regrets returned to the forefront of my mind. The possibility that I'd met the actual artist from beyond the grave was a lot to ponder or even believe in. It was easier to push the odd experience aside and focus on the actual work instead.

Before I began to sketch then complete that blank section, I would need to clean and repair the first two. It was a time-consuming process but one I looked forward to. After the layers of dirt, grime, and salt were carefully expunged, I would have a clear understanding of the exact colors I would need to use for the minimal repairs that were isolated to the bottom few inches.

I tapped my fingernail against my thigh, mentally outlining the steps I would need to execute with care over the next few weeks. Each stage of the process would have to be photographed and cataloged. Once that was done, I would painstakingly apply a solvent to remove the dirt and salt layered over the fresco, a process that would take weeks. If I'd had access to a laser, I could have used that to save time, but I did not. So, solvent it would be.

I continued to mentally detail the plan I would take, calculating the steps to ensure I would have what I needed. Good thing the weather was cool, but it was not below fifty degrees, which would cause a problem with the solvent.

When I eventually had the fresco's surface cleaned, I would apply a solution to dampen the plaster surrounding the damaged portion along the bottom. When the plaster was ready to be manipulated, I would then tint some water to the shade I desired using tinted powders, applying each color where it should go in watercolor fashion. As it dried, the tints would adhere to the mural.

I took another sip of the cup of coffee I'd made before stepping outside then let myself back in to Francesca's residence. The canal-front home was just as beautiful inside as it was out. Eggshell walls with century-old trim dressed the open floor plan. Chandeliers dripped with light-refracting crystals, and wooden beams spliced the ceiling, adding warmth to the rooms. In the living room, there were floor-to-ceiling windows framed by sheer curtains. I leaned against the white marble kitchen counter, pinching the note Francesca left me between my finger and thumb, double-checking her instructions.

Of course, her penmanship was as exquisite as I'd come to think of the woman herself. In a flowy script, she instructed that I use the Trascendentale line of Venetian plaster and tints for repair developed by Il Verroccio and his brother, Arnaldo, which was originally used to create the mural.

There was an open tab at the local paint store for me to use as I saw fit for things such as paints or tools. I'd heard of the Trascendentale brand before—it was made exclusively in Venice, but I had yet to work with it. I finally had my chance, and excitement buzzed through me because of the project I would soon begin.

The only sense of disappointment I faced was that Francesca had noted she was unable to locate a preliminary sketch of what the artist had intended for the third panel. It was critical in a restoration when a section was missing because what I painted should be an extension of his hand, not my own.

That would be a bridge I would have to cross when the time came. For now, I would take some before pictures then head to the paint store to purchase the solvent and supplies I would need. After a quick check of the time, I calculated that I had enough to take the pictures needed and place the order before heading out on the gondola tour Francesca had prearranged for me. A smile curved my lips as I took the first steps into the dream job that had brought me to the floating city I'd fantasized about for more years than I could remember.

After I took the pictures, I made a quick breakfast. With a slice of toast in hand, I was off to place the preliminary order at the paint store, arrange to have it delivered, then meet with my tour guide and be captivated by the sights.

Sunlight sparkled off the ripples of the canal, disturbing the mirrored images of the buildings as the gondola glided silently along the water. Antonio, my gondolier and tour guide, pointed out different landmarks and provided a truncated history lesson for each spot. Tilting my face to the sun, I closed my eyes and let the magic of Venice burrow under my skin for the briefest moment.

"We're near the end of our time together, Gianna."

I started from the gondolier's voice. My mind kept wandering back to the night before, to Giovanni and how he'd thought I was Sophia. Blinking the world back into focus, I grinned at Antonio. Francesca had been correct. I'd needed the tour, and my creative well felt full. "Thank you, Antonio. I loved it."

Pleasure warmed his dark-brown eyes at my praise. "You are most welcome." He glanced to the right. "Ah, we are here. Senora Marcello requested that you stop at Osteria Al Squero and have lunch before heading back. It's near the Rialto Bridge and the Marcello residence. Do you know your way?"

I spotted the bridge I'd crossed the night before that had made me queasy, its wrought iron pattern and arc etched in my memory. "I do. I'll be fine."

Antonio adjusted our direction, and we glided alongside a small dock. *Oh.* Terror washed over me in a tidal wave of unexplained emotion, and I gripped the side of the boat. A blinding headache and rush of intense dizziness hit me with no warning whatsoever.

"I'm back," a woman's voice said with a sigh in my ear before another bout of vertigo surged.

I gasped as the discomfort increased. *I'm going crazy.* I bent over, clutching my stomach with one hand and my head, which felt as if a hot iron seared it, with the other.

We stopped our forward momentum, and through my

lashes, I glimpsed the café. Canal-side tables filled the space, and I sucked in air. In the background, I heard faint voices of Antonio and someone else asking if I needed assistance, but I couldn't respond, as my body was frozen in agony.

A deep voice floated through the waves of pain and misery. "Is she all right?"

None of it made sense. *Am I sick? Jet-lagged?* I had been fine just moments before.

Two male voices murmured above me, but I couldn't focus on them because of the sensations that continued to pummel my body. Black dots swam before my eyes, and I listed sideways. *I'm going to fall into the water.* Fear prickled through me as I prepared for the cold water to envelop me. There was nothing I could do. All my strength had fled.

Strong hands lifted me then passed me to another pair. With the world spinning around me, I couldn't focus on faces. As my body left the gondola, the strange sickness ebbed, and an odd sense of peace fought the onslaught of raw terror and pain.

In the arms of a stranger, I took comfort.

I blinked as the worst of the discomfort eased, and as he angled his head toward me, I swore I recognized him. It was the same connection, longing, and deep familiarity that I'd experienced last night. The man who held me was the same one from the dreams that had reoccurred throughout my life. I would have known him anywhere. It *had* to be him. With a shaky hand, I traced his angular jaw, wishing he would press his lips to mine. "Giovanni." His name slipped from between my parted lips in a whisper.

He murmured something that I couldn't grasp, so caught up in the experience of being in his arms, as if he was my other half. For the first time in my life, I felt complete. But as my vision cleared, I realized he wasn't who I thought he was. He had the same angular jaw, deep mahogany hair, and intense eyes, but his were brown. That wasn't the only difference. I sank my teeth into my lower lip, confusion swirling through my foggy brain.

I became conscious of his hard chest, which I was pressed against as he wound through the tables with me in his arms. *Oh God.* "I'm fine. You can put me down." Heat flooded my face, and I knew my cheeks were red with embarrassment. But even as I said it, I didn't want to leave his embrace. There was such a sense of comfort there, and I innately knew he would keep me safe. My body betrayed me—even my fingers curled around the fabric of his shirt as if I didn't want to be let go, directly defying my words.

With each second, my vision focused, and the spell that existed between us dissipated. I became excruciatingly aware of where we were and of the people at the nearby tables, who watched our progression with open curiosity.

We passed a four-top where one of the women stood, laid her hand on his arm, and asked whether he knew me and if I was all right. He shook off her touch, his response a curt "I believe so, Lucia." Thankfully, she rejoined her friends, but I shivered at the possessive chill of her icy gaze.

He took a few steps then lowered me into a chair. The scrape of metal against stone was loud as he moved another close and sat next to me. Mortified, I took a deep breath then lifted my gaze to meet his. Warm cognac-colored eyes, not gray ones, met mine. Maybe he wasn't Giovanni, but he was just as captivating.

As he placed the back of his large hand against my forehead, he peered at me with concern. I couldn't help but stare. He looked familiar, but I knew I was fooling myself. I'd never met him before.

His mesmerizing eyes drew me in, eliciting an emotional response that I had no explanation for. I felt a connection that couldn't be denied.

He wore a dress shirt that pulled tautly across his broad shoulders, which were clearly layered with muscle. I knew because I stared. I should have been ashamed, but I was too raw to guard my thoughts and actions. In my dazed state, I swore he was sculpted after a god and brought to life. His face mostly held my focus, though. The chiseled perfection of his features and even the slight crook in his nose, as if it'd been broken a time or two, sent another wave of heat to my already flushed skin.

"You don't have a fever." He frowned, and I snapped from my stupor.

"I'm fine, really." I waved at the gondola. "My purse is still on the boat." I'd left it and my phone on the seat beside me, as I'd been snapping pictures while I toured the city with Antonio.

A corner of his alluring lips tilted into a charmingly crooked grin, and my gaze went to the dimple I knew would appear. But that made no sense. I'd never met the man before. I shook my head. I needed to get control of whatever was happening to me. First, the intense waves of nausea and pain, and then the uncontrollable attraction… it was embarrassing.

He lifted my purse and phone from the table. "They're here. You didn't lose anything." He flagged a waiter and ordered another coffee and water. "Now, tell me what that was back there."

"I have no idea. This is really embarrassing." I tucked a strand of hair behind my ear. "I've caused you enough trouble. Thank you for helping me, but I need to get going."

He chuckled. "Why don't we start again? My name is Sergio, and I'd be honored if you'd stay and have lunch with me."

"It's nice to meet you, Sergio." I glanced at my clasped hands in my lap as heat stole over my cheeks, and I nibbled on my lower lip. For some reason, I wanted to spend more time with him. "I'm Gianna. Are you sure you have time to eat with me?"

His warm expression accentuated his handsome features further. "I've only had coffee. I was about to put an order in."

I had planned to eat there anyway. "I would like that. Thank you." We took a moment to look over the menu, and I hoped he would drop the subject of why I'd almost passed out, but I wasn't that lucky. We placed our orders before he cast a weighty look at me that snapped my spine to attention.

"I'm a neurosurgeon. It's in my nature to be concerned about your well-being after an incident like you've just had. Have you had these symptoms before… or any others?"

Oh wow, a neurosurgeon? "I'm fine, promise. It was a weird thing. Probably jet lag."

He held up a finger to stop my protest. "Please humor me, because that didn't look like nothing a few minutes ago."

The waiter returned with my coffee, a glass bottle of water, and a cup he filled table side. The heady, rich aroma of the coffee teased my nose, and I automatically wrapped my hands around the saucer. I took a sip and eased back in the chair. *Maybe I should confide in him, just in case something is truly wrong with me.* "Are you sure you have time for this?"

He flashed that grin again along with a nod, and I caught myself before sighing. I needed to snap out of it.

"I don't have to leave for a meeting for a little while."

"All right, then. To be honest, I'm not sure what's going on. Maybe I'm sick? I really don't know. Since arriving here yesterday, I've had an odd bout of nausea and another accompanied by pain that came on suddenly. I'm not prepared, and then the sensations disappear just as they arrive, with a swiftness that's dizzying."

He asked questions, and I answered but mostly gazed into his deep-brown eyes. I wanted to paint him.

It was rare that I fell ill and even more so that I willingly went to the doctor. I waved away his medical questions—it was probably just some weird virus. The truth was that I wasn't his problem, and I doubted that I would see him again for the duration of the time I was in Italy. I twined my hands together under the table. It was time to be honest with myself. I wanted to see him again.

Our food arrived, and silence settled between us for a few seconds as we ate. The four women at the other table stood, gathered their purses, and wove through the outdoor tables. The one who had spoken to Sergio pierced me with a glare before she murmured goodbye to him. It shouldn't have bothered me that she ignored me, but it did.

"Are you visiting Venice, Gianna, or moving here?"

The warmth in his voice was back after a clipped response to the older woman, and it did much to alleviate the irrational emotional reaction I'd had to her. "I'm here to do some restoration work. Then I'll head back home to the States. So I'm not quite a tourist, but as I'm new to the area, I guess you could say that I am one."

"Well, I'm glad to have met you."

"You're a Venetian native, then?" I hoped so, because I wanted to run into him again.

"Yes. I've spent many years here, more in my youth. You'll love it, and I would be happy to show you around if you would like."

"That sounds amazing. Thank you for the offer."

He pulled a business card and a pen from his pocket. After writing something on the back, he handed it to me. "This is my card. If you don't mind giving me your number, I can ring you when I'm back, and we can do some sightseeing."

I readily agreed and typed my number into his proffered cell phone.

"I put my personal number on the back as well as the name of a local doctor in Venice. You should follow up with the doctor at the very least and have some tests run."

I gave a noncommittal nod to the doctor part. *Doubtful.* After glancing at his name, Sergio Vitale, I tucked the card into my purse. "Thank you again." Despite his charming attention, the reason for it was embarrassing. "I should go, and I'm sure you have to get to your meeting."

After a glance at his watch, he grinned, flashing a dimple on the right side of his olive-toned cheek. "I have some time. Why don't you stay and relax awhile longer? I could use the company. The rest of my day is full of meetings that I'm not looking forward to."

I smiled back. *In that case...* "So you don't live here?" I got myself under control and focused on enjoying the company of a handsome man in a place where I knew virtually no one.

"In part, I do. I travel back and forth between Rome, where I have an office, and Venice, where I have family."

Of course, he has a wife. "You're married?" I glanced at his ring finger. "Do you have children?"

"Neither." His eyes flashed with mischief. "My aunt owns a place here that's been in our family for generations. When we are able to get away, we come here. My brother, his family, and our parents stay as often as they can. We're a close-knit group. Venice is my home away from home."

"That must be wonderful."

He nodded. "How long will you remain in Venice, Gianna?"

"A few months. The restoration is a dream job, and already, the city feels like home."

A sincere smile lit up his face, and I sucked in my breath. In the back of my mind, I toyed with the thought that he was flirting with me. *Please be flirting with me.* I would be busy during daylight hours, but it would be amazing to have someone to go out with at night.

"Venice has that effect. I suppose that's one reason why I find myself here every chance I get." He took a sip of his coffee.

It was probably forward, but I was curious. "How do you come to Venice so often if you're a surgeon?"

"After six years of working long hours, I decided to cut my hours to part-time. I try to spend part of the week here and the rest in Rome, when I have appointments or surgery scheduled. It isn't perfect, but it's getting closer to what I'm hoping for."

I digested what said about his career, doing the math in my head. I had a friend back home in the States who went to medical school, and while he was deciding on his specialty, he'd discussed the length of residency he'd have to do with each one. Neurosurgeons had to do a seven-to-ten-year stint. Seven years put him at about thirty-three after his under-graduate degree and then four years of medical school. So he was probably around thirty-nine.

"Do you know anyone here?"

Sergio's voice pulled me from my thoughts, and my gaze locked on his. It was as if the rest of the world faded. *I know you.* An errant dark curl stuck out from the side of his hair, and I wanted to smooth it back. I blinked quickly, trying to dispel the odd trancelike moment between us. *Why is it as if I know him?* "No. I arrived last night."

"Well, now you know me." He glanced at his watch again. "I have to be going, but I'll be back in a few days, and I'd love to take you out sightseeing."

Yes. A thousand yesses.

CHAPTER 3

I spent the remainder of the day getting acquainted with the mural and the Marcello home. Excitement buzzed through my veins, chasing away the exhaustion of acclimating to a new time zone, but it caught up with me, and I'd gone to bed early. I woke the next morning with anticipation pinging through me because it was time to start repairing the mural. With a cup of coffee in hand, my gaze feasted on the supplies the paint store had delivered: the Trascendentale tints as well as the solvent and all the supplies I'd ordered. I spied the note Francesca had left for me on the counter and, not far from it, Sergio's business card with his cell phone number, which he'd given me the day before.

Before I could talk myself out of it, I sent him a quick text to thank him again for rescuing me and to let him know that I was feeling much better. With that taken care of, I got to work prepping for my day of repairs to the fresco waiting just outside.

I readied the solvent that I would need to clean the surface of the mural. Once everything was in order, I stood before the mural, letting the image welcome me into its essence before I focused on the section where I would start.

At the first touch of the solvent to the masterpiece before me, I was lost in a world not of my own making. Hours flew by. The sun climbed high in the sky only to begin its descent before my mind stirred at the grumbling insistence of my stomach. I'd had enough sense to pause for lunch, but it was nearing dinner. With the fading light, it was time to call it a day. I cleaned my tools in the farmhouse kitchen sink then got everything situated for the next day. I made a sandwich, washed it down with Pellegrino, then returned outside to survey my progress.

Movement near the canal caught my eye, and I turned to find my eightysomething neighbor, to whom I'd waved at the start of the day. She was once more sitting at a quaint wrought iron four-top table near the bridge and walkway between her home and the Marcellos'. She tempted me to her side with an offered glass of red wine. A smile curved my lips. I couldn't help but return her infectious greeting and accepted the request to join her.

"Ah, Bella, you must be the American Francesca told me about."

Amusement tinged my response at her nickname, which meant "beautiful." "Yes, I'm Gianna Bellini."

Long silver hair tumbled in an artful arrangement of smooth waves over frail shoulders that she'd wrapped in a shawl. But what held me captive were her warm, sparkling eyes and wide smile, set in a classically beautiful face that age only enhanced. A league of broken hearts must've lined the path to her doorstep.

"Care to join an old woman for a glass of wine?"

"Why not?" A smile curved my lips, and I dusted my hands off on my jeans before taking the seat next to her.

"Italian-American?"

At my nod, her features softened.

"My mother was born in Tuscany before she and her family moved to the States."

"Wonderful countryside." She lifted her glass then took a sip. "Caterina Brambilla. It's a pleasure to meet you. How are you enjoying our enchanting city?"

"So far, I haven't seen nearly enough of it, but I'm caught under Venice's spell. I'm looking forward to taking in the sights." I inhaled the scent of cherries and spices then sipped the red Sangiovese, savoring the warmth that coated my tongue in bold black currant and oaky flavors. Lovely and well-maintained flower boxes adorned the windows, and potted plants added pops of red to the corners of the small dock for Caterina's canal-side home. A living herb garden scaled the wall's side from the floor to shoulder height.

"It's lovely here." I leaned back, mimicking the aging beauty's posture before me.

"That it is, Bella." She reached across the table to give my hand a brief squeeze. "I'm enjoying watching you restore Il Verroccio's masterpiece and look forward to your interpretation when you create the missing section. It was a shame he never completed it, but when he lost the love of his life, there was no will to go on."

The original artwork was from the early 1900s, and there was no way Caterina would have known him personally. Still, the sadness that clung to her at the mention of loss told of personal experience.

"My husband passed away well over thirty years ago. I, too, understand what it's like to survive in a world without the love of your life. Not an easy feat."

"I'm so sorry, Caterina." My heart bled for the pain that flashed in her dark eyes.

She brushed aside my condolences with a flourish. "Call

me Cat, Bella. That's what my Lorenzo did, and it makes me feel closer to him."

I nodded, agreeing to use her shortened name and enchanted by the nickname she'd assigned to me. Her calling me beautiful wasn't anything I would complain about. We sipped our wine, chatting about the flora she lovingly cared for that made her small private dock so spectacular. Conversation floated amidst the gentle ripples of the canal as a gondola glided past. We lifted our hands in a wave to the passengers.

We soon spotted three people crossing the bridge, who called out a greeting to Cat.

"Ciao, Cat," an older woman with bold streaks of gray and features pinched in distaste murmured, and I sat up straight, recognizing her voice from my mishap at the *Osteria Al Squero*, when I'd nearly fainted after my gondola ride only to end up in Sergio's arms.

"Lovely evening, Lucia. Come, join us." Cat's raspy voice lured them closer. When they were on the private dock, she made introductions. I recognized Lucia's haughty dark-brown eyes and shoulder-length hair that fell in big curls to surround a face aged with regret. Diamonds dripped from her ears and hung from her neck. A rather large two-carat one flanked by rubies took residence on her finger. I repressed a shudder when her bony hand clasped mine.

Her daughter, Daniela, was close to my age and had a friendly face. Her long light-brown hair swung as she leaned forward to accept a glass of wine eagerly. But it was Lucia's stepson, Adriano, with his soulful eyes, high cheekbones, and olive skin who drew my gaze. Long thin braids covered his head and fell in ropes to frame his captivating features.

Lucia snared me with a false smile. "We've met, in a way. Have we not, dear?"

I nodded, mumbling, "Yes. At the café."

"Hmm, where my Daniela's Sergio rescued you."

"Do tell." Adriano shifted closer, giving my shoulder a squeeze. His warm support was quite the contrast to the frigid Lucia.

Daniela rolled her eyes. "We went to dinner a couple of times, *Madre*. It wasn't anything big. It's not like he's mine."

"There is something there, Daniela. Do not be so dismissive. A marriage to Sergio will be in your future. I am sure of it," Lucia said as if reprimanding.

"Ah, I don't think so." Daniela's features turned a bit green. "We are not as compatible as you seem to think. Besides, he lost interest, as he always does with relationships after a few dates." Under her breath and to Adriano, she muttered, "Not happening. Not marrying him."

"That's nonsense. He's just busy. You need to see it through." Lucia leveled me with a stare that dared me to deny her words, as if they were meant for me alone. "It would be a shame if history repeated itself."

What does she mean by that?

In a fortifying guzzle, Daniela drained half her wine. I could relate. Just being in Lucia's presence set my nerves on edge and made me want to run far away. Instead of acknowledging the odd dynamic between mother and daughter, I focused my attention on Adriano. My gaze crawled over his features, and my fingers itched to paint him. Before the end of my visit, I would capture both Adriano and Caterina on canvas. They were too captivating not to.

He lifted an eyebrow, amusement present in the curve of his lips. I pulled myself from my thoughts and answered his earlier demand for details about what had happened with Sergio. "It was nothing, Adriano. I had an odd dizzy spell, and Sergio kept me company until I felt better."

Disappointment came out in a huff. "You're holding back.

We'll get together for drinks soon, and you'll share every-thing." He patted my hand, and Daniela smirked.

"If David is there, she won't have a choice." Linking arms with her brother, she put space between herself and her mother. "When his boyfriend hears about Sergio rescuing you, he'll badger you until you fold and divulge all the juicy details. It's impossible to deny him anything."

"This is true." Adriano tapped his sister on the nose, elic-iting a grin from her.

"Well, this has been enlightening"—Lucia plucked the wine from Daniela's hand—"but we must be going. It was nice to officially meet you, Gianna." She bent and brushed a kiss on Cat's cheek.

"We'll be seeing you." Adriano squeezed me in a hug before he and Daniela both said their goodbyes to Cat.

When they were out of hearing distance, Cat's raspy chuckle eased the tension that had formed between my shoulders. "Pay no attention to Lucia. Status has always been important to her, and her prickly attitude is from being in an estranged relationship that she will never give up on." Her smile fell away only to be replaced by what appeared to be bone-deep sadness. "Her husband is the father of both Daniela and Adriano, but Lucia is only Daniela's mother. If it weren't for the love Daniela and their father, Marco, have for that talented boy, I would have worried about him growing up in that house. But that's a story for another day."

"Talented?" My interest piqued. I assumed the story she mentioned was about their home life, not his unknown-to-me gifts.

"Ah, yes. He's an exquisite tailor with a flair for period costume design. He owns Adriano Atelier studio with his longtime lover and business partner, David."

"Well, it seems I have a future date with the two of them for oversharing and wine."

Rich laughter poured from Cat, adding some color to her cheeks. "They are divine. They visit with me frequently, and we have the best time. Hopefully, you young people will include me during story time. Perhaps the three of you will visit here on my little patio?"

"I'm sure that can be arranged." *How lucky am I to have met such an endearing neighbor, with whom I can spend an hour or so with in the evenings?* Already, I adored her and Adriano's infectious personalities. Besides bristling at her mother's controlling ways, Daniela seemed like she would be fun too. Having met all of them would make it even more difficult to leave once the project was done. I twirled the stem of my wine glass as the sky darkened and fog rolled in on spidery legs and wafting tuffs.

"Our legendary fog." Cat broke the contemplative silence that had fallen. "It invades many a night as the seasons change and grow cooler. You must stay vigilant of your surroundings. We've had handfuls of tragedies where inebriated tourists or lovesick souls have gotten lost in the fog and perhaps forgotten that there are passageways that end abruptly in the canals. They walked off the edge of the path and into the arms of the canals."

I shivered at the picture she painted. "That's a warning I'll pay attention to." I drained the last drops of wine and declined Cat's offer of a refill. We watched as the fog permeated the air around us and seemed to pause near the part of the mural I'd worked on earlier.

"That's interesting." Cat murmured. "Perhaps Il Verroccio has come to oversee what you've done to his mural."

I'd heard the legend and marveled at the stellar condition of the artwork. There could have been some truth to what Cat said. "Perhaps."

"That's the beauty of Venice, Gianna. Time stands still, and we walk hand in hand with the ghosts of the past."

The fog and her words reminded me of meeting Giovanni the night before, and I wondered if that would be our one and only encounter. A wave of fatigue wafted over me, and I stifled a yawn that her sharp eyes caught.

With a gentle smile, she patted my hand. "Well, Bella, it's time for this old woman to go inside before the night's chill finds its way into my bones."

I stood as she gained her feet. "Can I help you with anything?" I gathered the empty glasses and bottle of wine as she made her way to the door.

"Just set them on the counter inside, to the left of the door." She encircled me with her thin arms in a gentle embrace after I completed her instructions. "Be sure to stop by often. I enjoy the company."

I promised her I would, and after shutting her door, I retreated to the Marcello residence and let myself inside as another jaw-dropping yawn consumed me. Bright eggshell walls greeted me along with the large floor-to-ceiling canal-side windows framed by tan drapes that pooled at the floor. The wooden beams that ran the length of the ceiling in evenly spaced rows added warmth to the spacious living room. With the door locked behind me, effectively shutting out the fog, I turned on a few lights and picked up my iPad, planning to do a little reading before bed. Alone with my thoughts, it was impossible not to think about the handsome man who'd held me in his arms the day before, after my gondola tour.

CHAPTER 4

$\mathcal{I}$'d thought that reading before bed would ease me into sleep and take my mind off of, well, everything. Curled up on one of the cream couches with a tan throw over my legs, I set my book aside after reading the same paragraph in a romance novel three times, unable to focus. A sense of contented exhaustion beat at me that evening, and I pulled my hair from the messy bun I'd fashioned so the long strands wouldn't get coated in solvent as I worked. I ran my fingers through the length, easing the tension from my head while my day skipped through my mind in pleasing panoramic frames. Working on the mural had been tedious and precise but also enthralling. Then I'd found a fast friend in Caterina and two potential ones in Adriano and Daniela.

Even with the satisfaction of a day well spent, my mind kept tripping back to the day before, the way Sergio had carried me away from the gondola, and how I'd first mistaken him for Giovanni. The mischievous sparkle in his dark eyes stole me, along with the way his irresistibly powerful presence oozed a sense of confidence and well-being. If I closed my eyes, I could still hear the deep timbre of his voice and remember how it had felt to be in his arms. A part of me wanted to. There was something inside me that was innately drawn to him.

After Lucia's attempt to warn me away, I felt compelled to seek him out. He'd given me his card. I could call him. Daniela didn't seem to share in her mother's opinion about their handful of dates. Of course, it would be better to speak with her about Sergio's availability or any claim she had to him without the presence of Lucia's dominating force.

The shrill sound of my cell phone pierced the silence, and I swiped it from the coffee table next to me. As if my thoughts had conjured him, Sergio's name lit the screen. I accepted the call before I could overthink it.

"Good evening, Gianna." The deep cadence of his voice sent a shiver dancing over my body. "How was your first full day of restoration work?"

The throaty chuckle that vibrated from my chest surprised me and heated my cheeks, something I was glad he wasn't there to witness. I had the strangest reactions to the man. "It was wonderful. I accomplished a lot."

"That's good to hear. And thank you for your text this morning about feeling better."

"Of course."

"I'll be in Venice soon and was hoping you would join me for dinner." Background voices filtered through the call as though someone spoke over an intercom. It sounded like he was at the hospital.

I could picture his face easily and longed to trail my fingers along his strong, angular jaw until he bent his head to brush his lips over mine. *Where had that come from?* He wasn't asking me on a date, just to dinner. "That sounds amazing, and it would be nice to have a friend to get together with while I'm here." With a shake of my head, I dislodged the traitorous image of kissing Sergio.

There was a tiny pause before he spoke. "I was hoping to take you out on a date."

"Oh!" *Wait a second.* I twisted a clump of my hair around my finger as Lucia's words rolled around in my head. *What if she's right?* I wasn't up for that sort of relationship. There was no indication from Daniela that she held onto hope to further a relationship with him, but Lucia's opinion still stung.

Besides, it was just dinner, and I was so attracted to that man. Even Daniela's mention that he was a bit of a serial dater couldn't deter me, although I'd had plenty of experience watching my father in action with a similar whirlwind attraction and his sudden loss of interest. He would marry quickly, followed not long after by divorce, only to repeat the cycle again. But I was projecting. I didn't know Sergio and would not typecast him based on a mother-daughter conversation.

My teeth sank into my bottom lip, and I pinched the soft throw between my fingers, rolling it back and forth. Excitement pinged through me. My decision was made. There was an undeniable attraction that sizzled between us, almost a tangible thing, and I wanted to explore it right then. "I—"

"Wait, hold that thought." Another voice trickled through the receiver, telling Sergio he was needed. "I have to jump into a meeting about an upcoming surgery. I'll call as soon as I can, and we'll revisit this. Until next time, Gianna."

I couldn't have stopped the smile if I'd wanted to. I made my way to my bedroom. Even though our conversation had been cut short, I would say yes the next time we spoke. The day had been a long one, and I needed to turn in for the night.

After getting ready for bed, I left the curtains and

windows open a crack to allow in the rippling canal's soothing sounds. With the sonic backdrop of the current's gentle flow, I snuggled beneath the covers. As the weighty pull of sleep lulled me, the frantic whisper of a woman dragged me into the depths of unconsciousness with one word—*"remember."*

CHAPTER 5

As if I had a snare around my neck, I followed the unknown woman's raspy whisper of "remember" as slumber welcomed me into its embrace. The duvet and plush mattress beneath me disappeared, and I floated. Lured into a sinkhole inside my subconscious, I sank through murky waters of cold despair until the sun shone overhead a hundred years in the past. It sparkled off the canal's rippling water and lit my path.

A bright flare illuminated before me in the shape of a woman. Before I could move, she rushed toward me. We collided then merged into one. My heart rate quickened. The thoughts I heard were hers. I was a passenger viewing her life through her eyes and experiences.

I walked as Sophia.

My fingers trailed past the unlit gas lamps and along the wrought iron railing as I stepped onto the bridge connecting my fiancé's home, the Dellucci manor, to the other side. Sketchbook in hand, I went alone with a design to capture the artist's likeness. He worked on the canal-side home's outer wall, directly across from where my parents and I stayed as the Delluccis' guests.

The artist across the way had snared my attention ever since I spied him while having coffee on the balcony with Signora Dellucci. He was devastatingly handsome and alluring and consumed my thoughts. But I was promised to another, and I knew in my heart that my obsession was unrealistic and troublesome. When I'd inquired who he was to Edoardo, my intended, he'd brushed off the artist I pointed out in his gruff, condescending, no-nonsense voice as someone not worthy of my time. However, his mother had shared the stranger's name—Giovanni.

Like a benediction, his name hummed through my consciousness with lasting effects. Too often, my gaze strayed. Several times, our paths crossed, but our interaction was limited, as I was not alone. Fortunately, Edoardo hadn't become suspicious. With his head caught up in his export business and its upcoming meetings, I breathed a sigh of relief as my infatuation grew and sought moments alone to stare as if moonstruck at Giovanni while he worked.

I'd finally arrived upon some luck. Both Edoardo's mother and mine were off having tea with a group of women their age, and somehow, I'd been left behind. Edoardo was away on business, as was his father. In truth, I'd only met his father at the beginning of our courtship—well, a forced entanglement, as the decision had been made by my family. It wasn't what I would have chosen for myself, but Giovanni was another story.

I peeked at the dashing man mere feet away. The pungent scent of paint urged me to inch closer, to admire the image he crafted on the outer wall. Charcoal poised over a blank sheet in my sketchbook, I soaked up the form of him, his broad shoulders beneath a billowy shirt open at the throat with his wide sleeves rolled up past his elbows, square jaw, and muscular legs encased in black trousers. When he turned, his gray eyes sent heat to dance over every inch of me. Hidden secrets and promises swirled in the dark depth of his sultry eyes, framed by enviable inky eyelashes. The side of his full, sinful mouth lifted in a crooked grin, and the hand that held his trowel stilled.

A sense of panic skated along my limbs, sending me back a hesitant step until he spoke and cast a spell that shot an invisible silvery cord straight to my being. His husky "mia bella" lassoed my heart, tethering me to him for eternity. I just hadn't known it yet.

The first step toward him erected an impossible-to-scale wall behind me, forever altering a destiny that I was helpless to deny. I uttered his name, and the fires of passion erupted in his hypnotic gaze and sent heat to climb through my rapidly rising and falling chest to settle in my cheeks. As I took the final step off the bridge connecting our two very separate lives, he closed the distance and boldly ran the backs of his fingers along the curve of my cheek.

"I've spied you across the way"—his husky baritone hit all the right notes and shut out the world around us—"my angel."

If only. "Sophia."

"Such an enchanting name for a beautiful woman."

From afar, I'd witnessed his interactions with others. Not once did he respond the way he did as when I was near. The attraction between us was tangible and undeniable. Deep in my soul, I knew it was a once-in-a-lifetime phenomenon, one I would give anything to have. I wanted him to go on, but I had to draw back, if only a little. "I've watched you work, and thought I would come to see, if you don't mind."

A mischievous sparkle lit his eyes, altering the smooth deep gray to stormy obsidian. "Please." His arm swept across the expanse of the wall with a flourish. "See the muse that has guided my hand."

With effort, I turned to gaze upon the fresco, following the play of light over the unfolding scene of a man and woman as they walked hand in hand over a bridge that spanned the canal. The atmosphere invited the observer to experience the building emotions between the subjects, and my skin heated with how she leaned toward him and his body angled ever so slightly to shield her. The image ignited something new and exciting in my heart.

I tucked my long dark hair behind my ears. The longer I studied the couple frozen in time, the more a sense of familiarity pierced my awareness. "Is it you?" Despite the view of his back, the man was clearly Giovanni's breathtaking form. I would have known it with my eyes closed.

"It is, indeed." He shifted so that his much larger frame brushed my chilled shoulder, and I borrowed from his radiating heat. "Look closer. What else do you recognize?"

As he urged, I shifted from the male figure's commanding presence to the woman. "Oh!" With an involuntary step forward, I visually traced the curve of her back, the dark, glossy hair, and the tilt of her head. Nervously, I shifted my focus across the bridge with the unlit gas lamps at the ends to the foreboding manor I would reside in until that fateful day I would say an obligatory "I do" to seal a business deal my father had orchestrated through my match. "They'll know."

Dread laced the statement. The Dellucci family was not a tolerant one, and in their eyes, I was their property. At the gentle touch under my chin, I allowed him to tilt my face back to him.

"People rarely see the treasures before them. Trust me. They won't."

A sheen of tears weighted by fear and regret coated my eyes, and my heart beat against my ribs as his gaze shifted from my eyes to my mouth. Helpless to resist, I inched toward him, laying the palms of my hands against his solid chest in a touch so forward I should have been scandalized. But with him, I wasn't. The contact between us felt like I was coming home, as though he was my world. Everything about the moment was right.

As he bent his head, closing the distance between us even more, my eyelids fluttered, and I tilted my chin up to give him access. He pressed a gentle kiss to my forehead, my cheek, and finally to the corner of my mouth, and everything in me sighed. More than anything, I wanted to shift enough so that he would take my lips in a kiss, but too many things held me immobile.

It was our first time meeting alone, yet it was as though he had been mine forever. I knew him deep in my soul. I could never forget him or deny him anything. In the span of a few stolen moments, he'd become my world.

What had transpired between us couldn't be undone, and I wondered if the gods would indeed smile upon us or smite us for all we dared.

The shrill ring of my phone tore me from Giovanni's arms.

I blinked through a hundred years then gasped awake, feeling the loss with an ache I didn't think I could ever expel. Slowly, my surroundings came into focus. Gone was the enchanting moment where Sophia had met Giovanni. In the place of their forbidden romance was Francesca Marcello's first-floor bedroom with its off-white Venetian plaster walls and exquisite furnishings. As more reality seeped into my groggy and resistant mind, I spied the source of what had pulled me from Sophia's sensual voice and Giovanni's alluring presence. From the bedside table, my phone continued to ring.

Without looking at the number on the screen, I answered.

"Gianna, were you sleeping?" His voice layered over the remnants of Giovanni's, and I sat up in bed in an attempt to separate the two.

"Sergio?" A shiver coursed through me. I'd left the windows open the night before, and a chill seeped from them… or perhaps it was the unease of what was going on with me and why I was having such vivid dreams through the eyes of Sophia, as if I was her. To ward the chill away, I drew the fluffy duvet up. Light spilled across the floor, and the soft hum of voices floated in from the outside. "What time is it?"

"It's nine in the morning."

"Oh." I couldn't wrap my head around it. The dual reality

from the dream was too much for my mind to grasp, and I preferred to push away the unusual experience and focus on the present and who was on the other end of the call. A thrill raced through me the more awake I became. The husky timbre of his voice stirred the banked desire that existed whenever I thought of him. "Is everything okay?"

"Yes. I'm sorry I had to cut our conversation short last night. I was working at the hospital. But the reason I called was because I should be back in Venice later today and wanted to take you to dinner."

The aftereffects of possibilities and so much more from my dream still sizzled through my blood, and I couldn't deny how Sergio made me feel. "I'd like that." The words were out before Lucia's warning came back into my mind.

We wrapped up the call quickly, as Sergio was still at the hospital, and I had work to do. I threw the covers back and braved the cold to get ready for the day. There was a painting I couldn't keep myself away from if I tried.

CHAPTER 6

I stood before the exterior fresco, lost in thought mere hours after I'd woken from Sergio's phone call, when I'd agreed to have dinner with him that night. A fragrant breeze drifted off the canal and with it, the faint strains of classical music that someone, probably Cat, listened to. The music wove its enchanting story, easing away the tension of the day. I let the captivating chords of Vivaldi's concerto wash over me. As the muscles in my neck and shoulders relaxed and my breathing evened out, the distant voice of a woman urged me to join her. My body swayed, drunk in the moment, while my mind drifted a million miles away, traipsing back through time at the insistence of her voice.

"You must remember." It was a voice I was becoming accustomed to. It was her—Sophia.

A sliver of clarity came to my surroundings, and I found myself back on the bridge that spanned the distance across the canal from the Marcello home where I was staying and Lucia's property, the Dellucci residence. I felt someone take my hand, the touch insistent and firm. When I turned to see who stood next to me, I was gifted with Sophia's profile. Her long dark-brown hair tumbled down her back. The moonlight highlighted her lovely features. Almond-shaped brown eyes were framed in spikey lashes. When she met my gaze, fear etched her inky orbs. Her hand squeezed mine as a tremor ran through her, transferring to me. But it was her words that struck an answering chord of trepidation.

"You must beware. I'm not the only one who has returned." She notched her head to indicate the Dellucci home, and I heard the distinctive bellow of Edoardo, her fiancé.

On an exhale, I followed her gaze past the glowing gas lamps staving off the approach of dusk at the end of the bridge. An imposing male figure stood on a second-floor balcony. With arms spread wide, he gripped the railing. It seemed that he braced himself by the wrought iron structure, but I instinctively felt that his tight grip mirrored the failing tenuous restraint of his temper.

I wanted to fight her, to flee, because I knew that she wanted me to experience something through her eyes. I was scared. There was a reason I had ominous reactions to that residence. I tried to take a tentative step back, but my body betrayed me, and after one pounding beat from my heart, I gave into the inevitable, at least physically.

My lips formed a silent "no" while hers betrayed us both with, "I'll be right in."

We moved forward, and with each step, I felt us merge into one. Again, I walked as Sophia to experience what she'd lured me into her world to see.

With each stride that brought me closer, I fought the urge to turn back for one last look at the small slip of walkway. There was just enough space for one person to precariously walk along the canal side of the Marcellos'. The narrow ledge led to the alcove where they entered via boat. The knowledge that my note was secure in the hiding place for Giovanni to find was the only thing that buoyed my spirit, flagging in response to my fiancé's summons.

Shoulders back, I forged on, stepped off the bridge, and made my way to the Dellucci's courtyard entrance. Once inside the door, I paused at the stairway to my left that led to the third floor, where I stayed with my parents. I hid my trepidation in the folds of my ankle-length dress, curling my trembling fingers between the skirt's fabric.

The silence on the ground floor accentuated the sound of my breath, and only tunnel vision got me from the door to the outdoor area, where I sat amidst the potted plants his mother had arranged to make the deck more inviting. I would not go to the family's private sleeping space on the second level, which Edoardo was well aware of.

I withdrew a deep-red bloom from the vase at the center of the table where I sat. The pad of my finger traced over the satiny petals. My heartbeat was loud in my ears, and I focused on slowing my breathing so that Edoardo would not sense my fear. He'd never done anything violent, but I was uneasy around him. My complaints and attempts to break the engagement had fallen on deaf ears. My parents were determined to establish a connection between our family and the Delluccis to further my father's business.

Despair lurked just beneath the surface of my placid expression. Pinching the flower, I plucked it away, a bruise forming on the delicate petal under my fingers. Hyperaware of my surroundings, I knew the moment he joined me. With effort, I forced a smile to curve my lips and greeted him.

"Sophia." He gave me a nod before taking the seat directly across from me, where the intensity of his gaze unnerved me even more.

"It's a beautiful night. I couldn't help but stroll onto the bridge to watch the gondolas gliding beneath it. Were you working?"

Silence met my question, and I wove my fingers together in my lap to hide the slight tremble that traveled through them at how he clenched his jaw. Barely leashed fury burned in his dark gaze, and I wondered what it would be like after we were married if I couldn't figure a way out of the commitment.

"A neighbor told me that you were visiting with Giovanni more than once."

I kept my features relaxed, despite the violent pounding of my heart. "I have. He is very talented, and I've enjoyed seeing the progression of the mural he's working on. Have you seen it?"

The air between us was heavy with the expectancy of his response. The longer his jaw remained clenched, the greater my unease grew. Had he found out about Giovanni and me?

"It is inappropriate for you to be in the presence of other men alone. I will not tolerate it." His fist struck the table's surface, causing the flowers to shiver. "Is that understood?"

My back slammed against the chair in a desperate attempt for space between us. At the moment of impact, I sensed my spirit leaving hers. Sophia had shown me what she wanted to, but I wasn't sure how to process it.

As my pulse returned to a normal rhythm, so did the centuries past, revealing the familiar sights of Giovanni's fresco and the Marcello residence where I stayed, courtesy of Francesca. The canal, not far from where I stood, shimmered with the reflections of a gondola gliding by.

I crossed my arms over my chest and pondered Sophia's words. *What did she mean that she wasn't the only one who had returned?*

CHAPTER 7

The swish of the water echoed in the small covered outdoor area where I sat tucked away as the evening—and my date—neared. A slight breeze ruffled my hair, loosening more strands than I liked from my bun. I tucked them behind my ears. *I love this alcove.* I'd found it while exploring the first floor of the Marcello residence.

A door off the kitchen opened to a private water gate that provided access to the Grand Canal near the Rialto Bridge. There was a small landing, or nook, several feet above water level that boasted a table and chairs for two and a lovely *trompe l'oeil* mural on one side of the wall, which lent a depth and lightness to the outdoor area. The new-to-me painting fooled the eye with its open, arched, tri-paned window overlooking pink-and-white window-box flowers and rolling sunlight-kissed waves of the Adriatic Sea, depicting a brilliant summer day. The image looked so real I expected to smell the heady, fragrant flowers mixed with salt air.

From the landing of the patio-like room cut into the villa, steps led to the water gate. My gaze alternated from the painting to the canal just beyond the wood and wrought iron doorway.

How have three days passed so quickly? Work was going well. There wasn't a tremendous amount of restorative work to do on the large partially finished mural on the outer wall of the building. Each panel of the painting blended into the next section in a panoramic scene. I was still stumped over the last unfinished scene and wondered what the artist had planned. A couple times, when I'd tried to sketch the phantom scene on paper, I drew a complete blank, which wasn't something I was used to.

I had to swallow a sense of defeat and call Francesca. Maybe she could think of somewhere the full sketches might be tucked away. Finishing my coffee, I went back inside. I would call her. I was supposed to begin the final panel in a few weeks, but I had nothing, no ideas at all. And the preliminary sketches weren't something I wanted to leave to the last minute to work on.

Wanting to stretch my legs, I let myself out of the house and headed along the sidewalk adjacent to the wall with the mural. I could stare at the fresco for hours. The artist had been very talented, and it was an honor to work on the mural. I wanted to make sure I did it justice by continuing his style in a seamless blend when the time came to paint the last scene.

With a final fleeting glance, I stepped onto the bridge and took my cell from my pocket. I pressed the button to dial Francesca. While it rang, I headed to the center of the small bridge. It spanned the distance across the canal from the Marcello home directly to the side of the building across from me. I flattened a hand over my queasy stomach. *Not again.* The random nausea was getting on my nerves. It must have been a slight stomach bug because the other explanation made no sense. The house on the other side of the canal would not have induced physical discomfort just from mere proximity. That was crazy.

"Francesca," I said as soon as she answered. "I'm so glad I caught you."

"Is everything all right, Gianna?"

I leaned on the bridge's railing. "Yes. I didn't mean to alarm you. I don't anticipate the restoration and completion of the third panel taking longer than a couple months." With the cooler fall temperatures, the curing process for the Venetian plaster would be slower, allowing me to work longer hours. I just needed to finish the cleaning process by the start of November, as the temperatures would drop. "I know you said you didn't have the preliminary sketches of the mural form the original artist, but I was wondering if you have any idea where I could attempt to search for them?" It was a long shot, as she had noted in our original communication that she couldn't find them, but I had to ask once more. The continuation of the artist's depiction was important to the restoration process and to me.

"Ah, if only we did have the sketches. You are welcome to look through some of his work displayed on the upper levels, but none is of the mural on the side of our home. We've searched before, but it is possible we missed something."

"Do you know who the mural depicts?"

"I do." Francesca sighed, and sadness echoed through our connection. "The artist is the man in the painting, almost a hundred years ago, and the woman he'd hoped to marry. They both died tragically before he could formally propose."

"That's horrible." I shivered at the thought of Giovanni and Sophia's lives ending in tragedy. I worried my lower lip, contemplating telling Francesca about my dream and the encounter with Giovanni. But I didn't want her to think I was crazy—I wasn't entirely sure I wasn't. As it was, she was sparse on details. I couldn't ask her for more. It didn't feel like my place. If she wanted me to know how they died, she would have told me. Maybe I could find the sketches in some of his other work.

"It's a story my family has passed down generation to generation, my dear. The last few decades have been different—the smell of paint and plaster has been missing on the eve of the full moon. About thirty years ago, the scent would be so strong along the sidewalk where the mural was painted that it was easy to imagine him there himself, making repairs. Not to mention that the mural was in pristine shape."

The sound of Giovanni's anguished voice as he called for Sophia came to the forefront of my mind, along with the way he'd looked at me as if I'd been there and the way I'd reacted as if I wished I were.

Giovanni's here. I wanted to tell her but didn't want to alarm her.

"Have a look upstairs at his work, and if you are having trouble figuring out what he meant to paint, my nephew, Gio, will be here in a few days. He has an uncanny ability to understand what our ancestor, whom we all call Il Verrocchio, envisioned. Such a talented boy."

"That's wonderful. I'll be sure to ask him when he arrives." I had to ask. "What does 'Il Verrocchio' mean?"

"It's a nickname that means 'the True Eye.' He earned it because he could paint anything he desired with such insight and emotion that his work spoke to everyone who viewed it."

There was the smallest pause. I wanted to ask more, but I didn't have to because she kept going.

"It's a shame he couldn't have seen his future—or hers. Before he died, he vowed to search for his intended wife through time until they could be together again."

It was such a powerful story. After another few minutes, we said our goodbyes, and I smiled at the gondolas sliding silently through the water beneath the bridge I stood on. Several minutes passed before I pushed off the railing to go back to the house.

Movement out of the corner of my eye stopped me in my tracks. *I'm supposed to be alone.* I trained my gaze on the second-story window. *Someone's inside.* The window was open a few inches. I hadn't gone up there. It wasn't me who'd opened it. *What am I going to do?* A brief silhouette of a person passed by the gauzy curtains.

It couldn't have been her nephew, Gio—he wasn't supposed to be there for a few more days. *But maybe? It could be him, or...* fear skittered along my spine. I didn't move. I kept my sight glued on the window, and again, a shadow moved behind the billowing white curtains. I nibbled on my lower lip, contemplating what to do. My eyes hadn't played tricks on me. The window was ajar. Someone was definitely inside.

There was no way I was going back in there alone. My hand gripped the wrought iron railing as I weighed my options. I took a hesitant step forward then stopped. Other than calling the police, which I didn't even know how to do in Italy, I didn't have any options. Besides, I didn't want to call them—not yet, anyway. Maybe there was a simple explanation. *Could Francesca have forgotten to tell me about a cleaning lady?* That would have made sense.

There was one person I could call. Instead of involving the police, I called Sergio. He was due back in town that day, and we had dinner plans. If he was in Venice early, maybe he could swing by and go through the house with me.

The phone rang once before he picked up. "Gianna, I was just thinking about you."

"I'm in a bit of a bind." I cringed at how high-strung I sounded. "Could you come by now?"

"Sure. I'd planned to ask you the same. I need to make it

an early night. I'm being called back to Rome for another emergency surgery consult tomorrow."

My gaze flicked to the second-floor window again. "I have a favor to ask. There's someone inside the place I'm staying at, and I'm standing outside, afraid to confront whoever is inside. Would you mind walking through the house with me? I'd rather not call the police, and I don't even know how to."

"Stay outside, Gianna," he ordered. "I'll be right over. Where are you?"

"The Marcello residence." I gave him the street address. He chuckled and I couldn't understand what was so funny.

The curtains moved back, and my gaze leapt to the window. Relief when I saw the familiar face made my knees weak. "Sergio?" Gio must have been a nickname his aunt used.

He leaned against the window frame, and I could just make out that sexy way his lips twitched as he said, "Must be fate."

Some of my anxiety faded after finding out that the person lurking inside the Marcello home wasn't a burglar. I stood motionless as the sound of a door shutting rang out. Then he appeared, tall, broad-shouldered, and so good-looking that my heart stopped for a second. His lips curved in a grin, and his face went from handsome to breathtaking. My heart beat against my rib cage, and I leaned against the wrought iron railing for support as my knees went weak with how much a single glance from him affected me.

With each step that brought him closer, my pulse kicked up a notch. Then he was in front of me, and the spicy scent of his cologne made me feel as though he'd wrapped me in a heated embrace. I fought against sighing in pleasure then dropped my gaze to the flowers in his hand. Waxy red rose petals tempted me to lean forward and inhale their fragrant smell. *Definitely a date*. If I'd had any doubt, I didn't anymore.

We faced one another on neutral ground, as I'd remained on the bridge. I hadn't moved, nor had my pulse settled—I was grateful that he'd said he would come to me. Good thing.

I hadn't forgotten how handsome he was, but I had let the power of his presence and its effect on me fade. I shouldn't have. It was a lot to take in, and I suspected it'd be easier for me to curb my strong reaction to him out in the open.

I wracked my brain for something to say after being so caught up in watching his approach. I shouldn't have worried because he broke the silence instead.

"My aunt should have told me that you were in residence last time I talked with her." His deep voice sent a rush of goose bumps along my skin.

I shrugged, trying to appear as if the incident hadn't affected me as much as it had. "She mentioned you'd be here in a few days, but I didn't connect how she calls you Gio, and then there's your different last name."

"My mom and Aunt Francesca are sisters."

"Ah, got it. The different last name from Marcello is due to marriage?"

He nodded, and I bit my lip at how awkward I was making things. Maybe if we went on a walk, I could relax a little. The house behind me, the one I'd dreamed about as Sophia and where Lucia now lived, gave me the shivers.

I shifted from the discomfort of the chill emanating from the Dellucci manor and infusing the space behind me in waves of dense foreboding as I peeked at the home over my shoulder. I rethought standing in view of their windows. If Lucia was inside, she had a clear sightline of me with the man she intended for her daughter, Daniela. And while I understood why Cat and Sergio said not to take her demeanor seriously, as her life hadn't gone as she'd hoped, I couldn't shake the apprehension I felt in her presence. At some points, I had an irrational shiver of fear. It didn't make any sense, as she couldn't do anything to me. Movement pulled me from my thought, and I appreciated another kind of shiver when my gaze landed on Sergio.

"It's a little early for dinner, but we could go on a gondola ride beforehand."

My shoulders relaxed, and I readily agreed. "Oh, wait. Your aunt said there were some drawings by Il Verrocchio upstairs. Do we have time for you to show me?"

"Of course. We can stop in the kitchen and put your flowers in a vase too." His large hand enveloped mine with the familiarity of longtime friends or lovers as he led me off the bridge, and I took comfort in the welcome sensation. Underneath those first-date jitters was an ease that only came from established relationships, a history we didn't have but was there nonetheless.

After we got the flowers situated in a vase he'd found for me, we climbed the stairs to the fourth floor, where Il Verrocchio's studio had been. The same large trio of windows as was on the first floor flanked the end of the room facing the canal. Floor-to-ceiling curtains covered them, limiting the amount of light filtering in. An easel stood off to the side, where my focus was drawn. I walked around the two couches that were positioned near the easel then stopped to gaze at the partially finished watercolor of what looked like the coastline of the Adriatic Sea.

My disappointment that the planned image for the third panel wasn't in plain sight was fleeting, and I felt a little foolish—Francesca had said she'd looked but hadn't found anything.

I felt the past settle around us. "Tell me about him. About why he and his girlfriend didn't have a happy ending."

Sergio shook his head. "Her family didn't approve of their union. Giovanni wasn't good enough, in their eyes. They wanted their daughter to marry the offspring of their old family friends. Their son was a businessman who did rather well in their exporting business. While quite successful, he was known to have a volatile temper and cared a great deal about the lofty status of his family and business. Despite her family's wishes, she did not love Edoardo."

"I wish their story had a happy ending." Knowing the outcome didn't stop me from wanting more for them.

Sadness swirled in the warm brown depths of his eyes. "Not for them. The alcove"—he waved a hand toward the stairs, and I pictured the outdoor patio with the private water gate—"had a special significance to them with the notes they left for one another."

"That's so romantic. Do you have any of the notes?"

"Yes. We have a few that were tucked behind the box and have taken them inside to preserve them as much as we can." He pointed out a couple frames, and I read one, a quick letter to meet late at night at the end of their bridge. "I suspect there were more and hope they turn up one day, especially their last notes before tragedy struck and they were found out. I'm not sure how Edoardo, her intended, learned of their secret liaison, but he did."

A shiver crawled over my skin at the idea of the two of them being found out. But I needed to pay attention, as I was on the fourth floor to find a hint about what Il Verrocchio had intended to paint before he died. We circled the floor while I peered at the framed pictures and easel without any luck before heading back downstairs. Once there, I let all thought of the work I would be doing fade and focused on the handsome man by my side.

"You mentioned a gondola ride?" I smiled at him, wondering how closely we would sit together on the ride.

"Yes." He grinned, and I forgot to breathe for a moment. "I thought we could head to Cannaregio for a drink and *cicchetti*. It's the northernmost *sestiere* of Venice. The district is one of the largest neighborhoods that tourists don't flood."

"That sounds wonderful." I grabbed a light sweater to

wear over my jeans and casual knit V-neck blouse when the air turned chilly after the sun set.

Sergio locked the house then took my hand in his again.

We chatted as we wound through the labyrinthine cobbled streets. It wasn't far, and before I knew it, we were in a gondola, enjoying a ride along the canal. It was picturesque, and I wasn't sure I wanted our time gliding through the water to come to an end. When we arrived, he disembarked and held out a hand for me.

"The *ristorante* is only about a twenty-minute walk from Piazza San Marco," Sergio explained when he caught me looking around.

"Oh, not far. Not that I didn't love the gondola ride, but we could walk sometime if we choose?" I was already anticipating the next time.

He nodded. "There are back streets we can take to avoid the congestion of tourists."

I instantly loved Ristorante Al Timon. The restaurant and surrounding area had a laid-back vibe. It was a beautiful night, and Sergio and I decided to sit outside at one of the canal-side tables. Old gondolas were moored to the side and refurbished to casually dine on, but they were at full capacity with a younger Venetian crowd.

The atmosphere was a much-needed break from the weighty sense of history that had shadowed my every step since arriving in Venice. We ordered a few cicchetti, side dishes, and a carafe of Soave white wine.

"Sergio? Gianna?"

We both looked to the side, following the voice. "Daniela," both Sergio and I said as we spotted her. With a quick glance, I noted the smile on his face—one without heat. His eyes contained nothing beyond a friendly greeting.

"This is fantastic, running into the two of you together!"

Her expressive eyes sparkled with mischief, and I had no doubt she would be chatting with Cat and Adriano shortly.

"Lucia." Sergio's voice held a faint chilliness to it, and my spine snapped straight. "I didn't know you frequented Ristorante Al Timon."

I didn't see her until she moved from behind her daughter. When she caught sight of me, her eyes narrowed, and a frown deepened the faint lines on her face.

"Well." Lucia's features pinched as anger heated her cheeks. "This is highly inappropr—"

"I had to drag her." Daniela cut off her mother's snide remark then looped their arms, taking a step away. "I just wanted to say hi. I hope you two enjoy your dinner." A knowing smile stretched across her face, and with a wave, she successfully pulled her mother away.

I'd watched Sergio's and Daniela's reactions to one another. It was clear they were just friends. I couldn't control Lucia, and it appeared that Sergio didn't care for the woman all that much, either. He started to say something, but the waiter interrupted us, which was probably for the best. I didn't want to waste time on our date with him talking about Lucia's behavior.

The waiter placed two sharable plates, one seafood and the other steak, on the table. Sergio lightly tapped the edge of the *florentina* steak served on a wood platter. "This reminds me of home, when my mother would entice my brother and me to help her prepare the vegetables and potatoes with the promise of steak."

"I love that. What was it like to grow up in Rome and visit here?"

"It was the best of both worlds." He took a sip of wine. "My aunt Francesca spoiled us, and the only way she got away with it was because my parents had so many friends on the island. When we came here, they had dinner parties or festivals to attend. As my brother and I got older, we would also go to the festivals, but we both loved the time we had with our aunt."

"Did you know Daniela and Adriano when you were growing up?"

"We did. As my brother is younger, he was closer to them. I hung out with a different crowd."

"Does your brother live nearby?"

"No. He and his wife live in Sicily with their two daughters."

I speared a potato. I liked Daniela—it was her mother that I was unsure of. *Why is it so important to her that Sergio and Daniela end up together?*

"Daniela and I are friends." His eyes sparkled with mischief, and a warm smile curved his lips. "I apologize for how Lucia behaved. She has her hopes tied to the image of my family and my career as the perfect match for Daniela."

I chewed the bite of potato then swallowed. The woman was determined. "When I talked with Cat, she said that Lucia's life hasn't turned out as she hoped." It was nosy, but maybe he could shed some additional light on Lucia's animosity toward me, or perhaps it truly was the threat of me dating the man she'd chosen as her daughter's future husband. "What was she talking about?"

He leaned back in his chair as a burst of laughter from one tethered gondola full of younger Venetians lightened the mood at least for a few seconds before the grim expression on Sergio's features penetrated the air. "Marco, Lucia's husband, fell in love with another woman. She was from France, visiting Venice to immerse herself in the art scene."

"She was an artist?"

The waiter stopped by and filled our wine glasses table-side before removing the empty plates.

"Yes. She was quite gifted. Several of her works are

around the city, and a buon fresco mural of Marco and her is on the building where she lived. Marco even purchased the building and gave it to his son when Adriano turned twenty-one. Someday, we'll have to go see some of her work."

"I would love that." A slight breeze rustled our discarded napkins, and I tucked the edge under my dessert fork. "I'm assuming this other woman was Adriano's mother?"

"Antoinette Cartier. I was young but old enough to remember her. She was stunning, and Marco was head over heels. Lucia refused the divorce, and when he and Antoinette had a child together, Adriano, he was rarely at home."

"Was Daniela born yet?" My heart broke for her, as it sounded like she may have lost her father during that time too.

"Yes, she is a year older than Adriano. The only thing Marco did right was making sure that he spent time with Daniela too."

"So what happened?"

"On the eve of Antoinette's death, Lucia agreed to consider divorce, but she wanted him home that night to discuss it. Marco left Antoinette at the restaurant they were dining at, promising to return to her that same evening with the news."

I leaned forward. "He didn't tell her he was negotiating with Lucia?"

"That, I don't know. I find it hard to believe he wouldn't have confided in her, regardless of what Lucia demanded. But from what I heard, there was a stipulation that no one knew what they were going to talk about."

"Then how did you learn about it?"

He grinned, and my mind went momentarily blank before I snapped myself out of it. "I'm getting to that. You need to know that Antoinette lived with their son in Cannaregio at the end of the Ponte de Chiodo bridge. It's one of only two remaining without a parapet. Most of the bridges in Venice were built without rails until the eighteenth century. Antoinette's is one of the two that were never updated. It was always a bit precarious, but at night it was very much so, especially when the fog rolled in."

I didn't like where the story was headed.

"When Marco arrived home, Lucia changed her mind. They got into a huge fight out on their balcony—the reason I knew about it was because my brother and I were in our room on the third floor with the windows open. But it was fate that night when tragedy struck. I'm not sure of the actual time, but Marco learned of Antoinette's untimely death. It's rumored that she took her own life."

"Really?"

"I don't think so, but that's the version of the story Lucia attests to."

"What happened to Adriano? I met him with both Daniela and Lucia."

"He lives in the Dellucci home, and both Marco and Daniela dote on him. Antoinette didn't have immediate family for him to live with. It made sense for him to be with his father, and at five years old, it was impossible not to love him. Lucia even tolerates his presence."

"Wow. And Marco and Lucia are still together?"

"In name. Her image is very important to her. I don't believe she would have ever granted Marco a divorce, but the need for it died with Antoinette, and Marco didn't want to be separated from his children. There is no love between him and Lucia."

"I'm in shock. Adriano and Daniela seem so well-adjusted."

"That would be Marco's effect. He spent every moment he could with them when he wasn't working."

"I guess I can understand Lucia's discontent." I meant

"bitterness" but thought the other was a kinder word. I drained the last few sips of my wine as the waiter stopped by our table with the bill. Sergio took care of it then offered his hand to help me from my chair.

"It puts things in perspective."

I made a noncommittal "hmm" to his statement.

"What did you think of the restaurant?"

"I loved it. It's my new favorite spot in Venice."

We walked the short distance to where he'd reserved another gondola to take us home. We sat side by side, gliding through the canal, our way lit by lanterns and lights from the surrounding buildings reflecting on the water's rippling surface. It was romantic and peaceful. When we alighted from the craft, Sergio linked my hand in the crook of his arm, and we strolled the rest of the way home, talking about composers and our love of classical music, especially Mozart and Vivaldi.

It wasn't until we arrived at the Marcello residence that the first stirrings of temptation entered the evening. We used the rear entrance, which spilled into the kitchen. Off to the side, stairs led to the upper levels.

I tugged my cardigan tightly around myself. "I'm not sure how we're going to live in the same space. Maybe I should get a room at one of the hotels?"

"No, you're meant to stay here. We'll make it work." Sergio turned to face me. The look, the heat in his gaze, stirred every fantasy of the man to life. He cupped the side of my face, and the pad of his finger brushed along my cheek, sending sparks of desire in their wake. "I won't invade your space while I'm here a few nights a week."

My gaze dropped from his stormy eyes to his lips. As he closed the distance between us, I swayed toward him. Every nerve ending in my body screamed for his touch, my reaction unusual but undeniable. We stood toe-to-toe. My pulse kicked up a notch, and all I could focus on was him and how I was helpless to resist what was happening between us.

When his lips brushed against mine in a divine, slow caress, I flattened my palms against his chest, spreading my fingers to touch more of him. The kitchen faded, and in his arms, the fantasy of him that existed in my mind intertwined in a burst of brilliant colors. The spell of the moment wove between us as if we had been transported to another time, bound by a kiss, capable of stopping the world on its axis.

CHAPTER 9

$\mathcal{I}$f I hadn't already known it, I wouldn't have realized that Sergio and I occupied the same residence. True to his word, he helped to maintain that illusion that he wasn't also staying there by using another entrance to come and go, so I had the full run of the first floor. We were both busy during the day, but at night, he would take me out to stroll along the streets of Venice, to experience it as a true Venetian. I loved all the old-world architecture and inviting cafes. As we explored, I could no longer deny my connection to the island, and I formed a tentative plan to move there. Next time I talked with Francesca, I would ask her about positions opening in the organization she belonged to that strove to conserve Venice's art.

While I cleaned up after working on the restoration, Sergio texted that he had a conference call to finish up, then he would be down, and we could go to lunch. Not wanting to wait inside, I exited the residence.

"Good morning, Bella. Won't you join us?" Cat called from her lovely dock, and I couldn't resist passing the time with her before Sergio and I went to lunch.

I made my way to Cat's canal-side table and chairs. Daniela and Adriano were sitting with her, having coffee. I breathed a sigh of relief at Lucia's absence. I wasn't in the mood to deflect snide comments, as my patience was quite thin. That third panel on the mural I would eventually begin to work on still eluded me.

Daniela lifted her hand in a wave, and I pulled out a free chair to sit with them, declining the offer of coffee from Cat.

"Aren't you stunning?" Adriano tugged at my loose braid, which fell over my shoulder. "Very French."

I grinned because I couldn't tell from my white sundress and half sweater wrap that my outfit indicated a region.

Daniela smacked her brother. "Her dress doesn't say France. You're dramatic."

Somehow, he managed to look down his nose at his sister before Cat interrupted.

"Daniela, don't be insensitive."

Her gaze swung to Cat's, and a silent conversation ensued before Daniela's eyes widened, and she turned to her brother, her mouth forming an O. "I'm sorry, Adriano. I wasn't think-ing." She flung her arms around him, mumbling again that she was sorry.

The three of them didn't say a word, and I wasn't sure what I should do. It was obvious that whatever they were dancing around was private. I tensed, ready to gain my feet when Adriano turned to me, sadness swimming in his eyes.

"The anniversary of *Maman's* passing is this weekend."

"Oh, I'm so sorry, Adriano. I didn't know."

"You did nothing wrong." He winked at Daniela. "It's always this one that sticks her foot in her mouth." He pulled out his wallet and removed a picture, angling it so that I could see the stunning woman holding a small child who was clearly Adriano. He and his mother shared the same olive skin tone, almond-shaped eyes, and thick ebony hair.

"She's beautiful."

He squeezed my hand then put the picture back in his wallet. Tears misted in his eyes before he blinked them away, turning toward the floral arrangement. He probably needed a change of topics. We all did.

Adriano fingered one of the waxy petals from the flowers Cat had set in a vase and on the table. "These are pretty. Are they from your store?"

A contented sigh left Cat's mouth as she gazed at the bouquet before she nodded. "Did you know, Gianna, that my sweet Lorenzo owned a flower shop not far from Adriano's business?"

"No… ah, so that's why your plants flourish under your care. Your outdoor space is so beautiful. If I was in charge of all this, they would not do as well or look so inviting." It was wonderful to sit amidst all the blossoms, which added to the atmosphere.

"Lorenzo planted many of them. Not a single one has given me an ounce of trouble. By the health of the flowers, I know he is watching over me even now." She dabbed at her misty eyes.

"Someday, you will be together again." Daniela patted Cat's arm then winked at me. "You should tell Gianna about some of Venice's superstitions. Cat knows them all."

"If you've lived as long as I have, it's impossible not to." The tears subsided, and a sparkle returned to her deep-brown eyes.

"Pff, you're a timeless beauty. There's no need for talk of age." Adriano flattered her before he turned to me. "Lorenzo was a frequent visitor of Palazzo Mastelli del Cammello."

"What's special about the palazzo?" I loved the stories and rested my crossed arms on the table.

Cat smiled then answered, "My dear husband attributed his success to touching the nose of the statue of Sior Antonio

Rioba. The simple act is believed to grant luck to your business affairs. But I never associated the superstition with his accomplishments. The man possessed charm and a green thumb."

Adriano squeezed my arm. "I've done this as well." He shrugged, that mischievous twinkle both he and Daniela had turning his eyes to a stunning amber. "But if you visit Doge's Palace, do not walk between the two pillars of the lion and dragon. The simple act will invite misfortune."

"He's right," Daniela interrupted. "Executions took place there for centuries."

"Mmm. This is true," Cat echoed. "No good comes from walking amidst tiles soaked with tragedy, blood, and death."

The shiver that passed through me wasn't from the air. "Oh, I'll be careful to avoid that path." That was the last thing I needed.

A gondolier glided by with a cheery, "Ciao, Bella." Our conversation paused while Daniela's joyful laughter filled the air, followed by her reply, "Ciao," back to the flirty, smiling man on the canal.

I took in the increase in gondoliers propelling their passengers through the water. "The canal is crowded today." A steady stream of gondolas passed by, and we returned joyous greetings.

"There is an influx of tourists with the masquerade event approaching," Adriano explained. "And with that, I must get to work before David comes looking for me." He winked then bent and kissed Cat's and Daniela's cheeks before doing the same to me.

"You have yet to tell us about your date. How are things with Sergio?" Daniela asked.

My cheeks flushed, and I fought the urge to fan myself before I darted a nervous glance at the Dellucci home. "We're getting to know each other."

Both she and Cat snickered before Daniela clued me in. "He's a beautiful man but not exactly my type. My mother is a hopeless matchmaker. Your worry isn't needed."

"I must be easy to read." I wished I'd taken them up on the coffee and eyed Cat's with an envious glance as she took a sip of hers.

Cat winked. "It's refreshing, dear."

Daniela grinned. "You don't have to worry about my mother. Anyone would be uneasy. It's my mother who's interested in him for me. Sergio and I are just friends."

"Thanks for telling me that." I mentally breathed a sigh of relief. I didn't need animosity from Daniela in addition to Lucia, who was bad enough on her own.

"So"—Daniela leaned closer, her voice dropping to a conspiratorial whisper—"what's it like living in the same house as Sergio?"

A warm breeze danced through the flowers that lined Cat's dock. I shifted my gaze from the pretty swaying petals to Daniela's inquisitive expression. "It's okay. He's been great about not invading my space and using another entrance to come and go to his floor."

"Such a gentleman." Cat set her delicate china cup on the saucer. "How long will we have you with us?"

"Another few weeks at least."

"Lovely." Cat smiled. "I believe Francesca will return around then too. It will be wonderful having all of you here."

Daniela scrunched up her nose. "Or awkward. If you find it strange to be under the same roof as both Sergio and his aunt, you could always rent a room. My mother mentioned that there's one available at Ca' Dario."

Cat speared Daniela with an unreadable expression. "Daniela, you must be joking."

Her brows furrowed. "Right… I didn't connect that reference."

Their coded words weren't making sense to me. "What reference?"

Cat patted my hand across the table. "You don't want to stay there, Bella. Ca' Dario is the cursed house. Merely walking by the house, you will sense the lingering darkness, the evil that lives inside its walls. Centuries ago, a curse on the manor claimed that its owners would befall hard times or death. And over the years, the rumors have been proven true. Pay no attention to what Lucia said. No one lives in that place anymore. There are no rooms for rent."

I wove my fingers together, the tight grip leaching them of color. It was obvious that Lucia hated me, and I couldn't be more grateful to have Cat on my side. When Sergio came out, I forced the tension in my limbs to ease and gave both women a hug before I met him halfway down the walk, eager to brush all talk of curses from my mind. After a final wave to Cat and Daniela, we left for our date.

Sergio clasped my hand in his as we walked down the street on our way to lunch. "You look beautiful, Gianna."

I tilted my head to meet his whiskey-colored eyes with a smile. "Thank you. How was your call?"

"It went well, and the best part is that I'm free the rest of the day. Aunt Francesca also phoned. I asked her how flexible she was with the mural timeline, and she assured me nothing was set in stone."

I shook my head, trying to dispel the irritation on his speaking on my behalf about my agenda. I wanted to spend more time with him, too, but my work was important, regardless of what I'd planned. "Are you trying to negotiate an afternoon off for me too?"

"Guilty." Straight white teeth flashed as he grinned.

I brushed aside the slight annoyance with a glance at the overcast sky. "It's supposed to rain later, anyway. I had thought to take it off and soak up some of the sights. I'm still struggling to figure out the third panel on the mural, which is what's left to do. Francesca mentioned you might have some ideas."

"Ah, I think I may have a solution to that if you wouldn't mind going to Rome with me in a couple of days?"

A crowd of people exited a bar we passed by, and he pulled me against him, wrapping his arm around my waist and settling it on my hip. "If it'll help me figure out the scene, then absolutely."

Soon, we were seated at a café near Piazza San Marco and placed our orders shortly after. Luck was with us, and not long after we received our drinks, our *tramezzini*, triangular Italian sandwiches, arrived.

"Why do you go back and forth so much between Rome and Venice?" *Oh, that came out wrong.* I opened my mouth to apologize, but he stopped me. His deep laugh rumbled from his chest.

"Aside from wanting to see my aunt, and now that you're here, Venice has a draw that I choose not to fight. My brother and I have fond memories of our visits. Aside from the high tourist times, like during the festivals, it's a wonderful place to be."

"I've heard how crazy it can be around the festivals."

"Hmm. There are some streets that bottleneck from the press of the crowd, and it's a claustrophobic nightmare. My brother refuses to come during that time of year, and we don't see him or his family as often as we'd all like. I don't usually stay for the festivals, either, but I thought I would make an exception to be here with you."

"That sounds like fun." The festival wouldn't occur for months. I doubted I would be there that long, unless I gave in to the strong pull Venice had over me and made the move permanent.

"When my brother and I were younger and not allowed

to go to the festival, we disobeyed our parents and snuck out."

"How old were you?" I grinned as I imagined Sergio as a young boy getting into all sorts of mischief.

"I can't remember for sure, maybe ten years old? We hadn't planned to stay out long and had swiped a couple of masks to fit in."

"I take it you didn't fit in?"

His deep laugh sent a jolt of warmth to my gut. "Not in the least. Perhaps if we had been taller." The smile on his lips fell away. "While we were weaving through the crush of people, I lost sight of my brother. We were almost at Piazza San Marco. I'll never forget the sense of fear and desolation that struck me when I realized he wasn't there. It was more, as if I knew something traumatic and irreversible would occur if I didn't find him."

I sat up straighter, my elbow slipping from the table. "But you found him?" He must have, but the stricken emptiness that flashed briefly in his gaze left a sliver of worry in me.

"I got lucky. When I backtracked, I found him. Only a few adults separated us. We went home after that. I had to drag him, but I was bigger, so it wasn't all that difficult, and I bribed him by saying that I would do his chores that week."

The waiter reappeared, and Sergio took care of the check before helping me from my seat. We exited the restaurant as another surge of people entered.

"It's jam-packed today." Part of me wanted to go back to the manor to avoid the crowds.

"It is. More tourists are arriving for a masquerade. The event is a silent auction. And with that in mind, I thought we could go make masks before that, too, is overrun by all the people arriving in Venice."

"That sounds like fun." We moved in sync, strolling through the piazza and chatting about our favorite foods, movies, and books until we were on the edge of the Piazza San Marco. A slight drizzle had started, but it didn't detract from the enjoyment of the afternoon.

When we came to a standstill in front of a mask store, excitement pinged through me. I knew what I wanted and couldn't wait to get started. Sergio had booked a private session, which allowed us to choose more intricate masks, from full face to demi, to work on.

The hour flew by, and I was thrilled with both of our creations. As we exited, I turned to him, the hand-painted, gold-leafed mask clutched in my hand. "Where are we off to next?"

Sergio's lips curved into a smile. "I promised Adriano we'd stop by. And as lovely as your mask is, I have to warn you that he might veto our masks in favor of ones that he made."

I shrugged, causing some of the hair that had managed to get loose from my braid to slip over my shoulder. "I'm okay with that. This afternoon was perfect, and I have a souvenir to remember it by."

His gaze darted to my lips. As he brushed my hair over my shoulder, his fingertips grazed the sensitive skin on my neck, causing me to shiver. He cleared his throat and pulled his hand back. "Are you ready to go?"

I didn't trust my voice and nodded instead. When we came upon Adriano Atelier, the period costume and tailor shop, I had to pick my jaw up from the cobbled street we stood on. The display window portrayed a scene from another time, its mannequins decked out in lavish floor-length silk gowns trimmed in all manner of intricate designs.

Sergio guided me through the door, the pleasant tinkle of the bell overhead announcing our arrival. There was a man finishing up a sale to a customer. His brown hair was on the longer side and brushed his collar. I offered a smile, which he returned, noting his bronze skin and pale-green eyes. I was innately drawn to his inviting charisma.

We hung back and waited, which gave me plenty of time to peruse the racks of dresses displayed throughout the store. In a wash of bold silks and satins, my mind went fuzzy around the edges, desperate to remember something just out of reach. My fingers caressed the pretty dresses as if it was the most natural thing in the world. Drawn to the dark-red gowns, I plucked one from the rack as my vision faltered. The elaborate gown wavered as my sight winked out. My head spun with dizziness. Everything before me faded, and a dimly lit room replaced Adriano's studio.

Soft light flickered from a bedside table as I brushed lint from the deep-red gown. With a twirl, giddiness fluttered through me in anticipation. I would see Giovanni tonight. If he agreed, the course of my life would change forever. He would want the same. I knew it with every fiber of my being.

Slowly, my gaze climbed up the full skirt until I locked onto my image in the floor-length mirror. The black demi mask dangled from my fingertips, and once securely in place, there was no hiding the sparkle in my eyes.

Senora Dellucci called from below, and I heard my mother respond. The three of us were going to the carnival tonight, only I wouldn't remain with them for long. They would soon be waylaid by friends, and that was when I would separate and find my true love.

Luck was on my side, as Edoardo had been delayed by meetings and would not be escorting us. With the mask firmly in place, I left my room in a flourish of silk and lace.

It wouldn't be long. I descended the stairs, and laughter trailed up to greet me, as did the flash of a camera's bulb.

I blinked the unexpected brightness from my temporarily blinded sight and jolted back into the present, no longer in Sophia's body or time. The shock of seeing her face in the mirror ricocheted throughout my mind—we looked so similar.

Sergio held onto my shoulders, his face inches from mine, worry causing a crease between his brows. "What happened?"

I leaned into him, letting him hold me with the dress crushed between us. "Just a little dizzy. I'm all right." But I wasn't, and a part of me longed to tell him what I'd seen.

His hand rubbed up and down my back in soothing circles. "We should run some tests, see what's causing you to have these symptoms."

"Mm." My response was noncommittal because I knew what caused the problems. I just wasn't comfortable with telling him, at least not yet. I didn't want him to think there was something psychologically wrong with me. I repressed a shudder and let the warmth of his body seep into mine. "I think we should postpone the rest of today. I need to rest."

Sergio readily agreed. Over my head, to a concerned David, he made our excuses, promising to come back another time. It seemed Adriano had a dress in the back that he'd told David would be perfect for me. I didn't move from the protection of Sergio's embrace. I couldn't. Witnessing Sophia get ready for the festival had unnerved me more than I wanted to admit.

Between our bodies, my grip on the gown was unbreakable and shaky as the knowledge of what I'd seen penetrated my consciousness. I knew beyond a shadow of a doubt that I'd worn a similar one before—just not in this lifetime.

CHAPTER 10

$\mathcal{A}$ good night's sleep should have helped dispel the unease of yesterday's vision, but it hadn't. With the back of my hand, I rubbed my forehead, trying to stave off the headache that threatened. I was tired, hungry, and a little conflicted about all the time I was taking off with Sergio. The day before had been an entire afternoon, which I'd enjoyed but worried over nonetheless. I was close to finishing half of the mural's cleaning. It was a slow process with the solvent and working with the utmost care, but I was pleased by how far I'd gotten.

The click of high heels sounded to my left. I turned to offer a greeting to find Lucia striding my way with determination. She paused in front of me, pursing her lips with a sour expression that made me feel judged. She found me lacking.

"Ciao, Lucia."

"Ciao, Gianna." Her gaze flitted over the mural, and I swore I saw fury flame to an inferno in her eyes. "How is the restoration going?"

My body was tense, and I forced myself to relax. "It's

going well. The cleaning process takes some time, but the repairs needed to the first two panels are minimal, which is good."

"Hmm. When it's done, you will return to the United States?"

Direct. "That's the plan."

She gave a curt nod then took a step around me. "Will you be staying for the masquerade fundraiser in November?"

"Oh, I don't know if I'm going to it." *Sergio hadn't formally asked.* "But yes, I'll be here in November."

A half smile curled her lips. "You should go to it. Francesca is involved in the planning, and I would assume she will be back to attend as well."

I bent and picked up the supplies for cleaning the mural, ready to head in and make lunch. "Thank you. I'll have to call her and ask about attending."

"Of course, dear." With a dainty wave of her fingers, she swept past me, toward the bridge that connected the walkway between Francesca and Caterina's properties, across the canal, and to hers.

I said goodbye, then, with my tools precariously balanced in one arm, opened the door to go inside. With one foot across the threshold, I spied Cat on her deck, watering. "Cat," I called, waiting until she turned. "Would you like to eat lunch with me? I can make paninis and bring them to your deck."

"That would be wonderful." Cat's smile eased more of the tension clinging to me, and I went inside and got busy preparing our lunch.

I stacked our sandwiches and fresh fruit on a tray, along with two bottles of Pellegrino. Balancing the tray, I left the Marcello house and closed the distance to Cat's deck, where she waited.

"That looks lovely, Bella."

I smiled at her nickname for me.

"I thought we could use some flowers for our meal too."

I set the tray on the table and leaned over to smell the bouquet of red blossoms in the center of the table. "I love them. It's perfect for our lunch." After placing our food and drinks on the table, I set the tray aside. Beethoven's *Fur Elise*, cello rendition, drifted through her open window and added to the ambiance. The canal shimmered beneath the sun like glass, and I longed to dip my toes in the water, even though it wasn't hot outside. I thought I might need a day at the beach, but I had too much to do to clean the mural.

Several minutes passed while we ate before she set down her sandwich and leveled me with a knowing look. "Something's bothering you."

I, too, set down my food. "Is it that obvious?"

She nodded. "Your shoulders are scrunched almost to your ears. And if you don't stop furrowing your eyebrows, you'll have a permanent line forming."

With the pad of my index finger, I massaged the spot between my brows. "I don't know what's wrong with my emotions today. They're all over the place, and when Lucia stopped for a few words, I... I don't know. I get such mixed feelings from her." It was more than that, though. It was as if it was engrained in me to beware of her. It wasn't something I was comfortable even attempting to verbalize.

"Waves of unhappiness often come off Lucia. I'm sure that's what you're feeling. She wears the weight of a failed marriage on her shoulders."

I huffed out a breath. *More like fury at my mere existence.* "I know she wishes that her daughter and Sergio would have worked out."

"She meddles. Daniela will do as she pleases, and Lucia will be forced to let her matchmaking scheme go. She probably has already."

"It's hard not to take it personally."

Cat pushed her long hair over her shoulder then leaned back in her chair. "Lucia has been this way for so long that most of us who know her overlook her sour disposition. She and Marco live in the same house but barely speak to one another. They are married in name only. It's quite sad. I'm sure Lucia thought she would get her husband back after his affair ended."

"When Antoinette died?"

"Yes. But it's as if part of him died with her. He was never the same."

"I'll work harder at being understanding with Lucia."

"That's all we can do." Cat picked up the remaining half of her sandwich. "Now, what else is bothering you?"

I had to laugh. *I must be an open book today.* "Meeting Sergio has been a whirlwind. It's difficult to describe, but there was this undeniable attraction… and at the same time, an ease between us, as if I'd known him all my life."

"That doesn't seem like a problem."

I twisted the lid to my bottle of Pellegrino, needing something to do with my restless hands. "No, it's amazing. The problem is that he isn't taking into account how much work I need to accomplish with the mural when he shows up during the day with a surprise to go out to lunch, which inevitably turns into an adventure through Venice." Heat stained my cheeks, and I snapped my eyes back to hers. "I love it. Don't get me wrong. I do appreciate his effort and spending time together."

"Is it because he called Francesca to get time off for you?"

"Yes. I feel petty about it; it's my job. I shouldn't be taking time off so I can go out with her nephew."

Cat's smile stretched wider. "Trust me, she's fine with it. I talked with her yesterday evening. Francesca wouldn't hear of you working if Sergio wanted to take you out. She dotes on her nephews and was thrilled about his keen interest in you. Didn't you meet her?"

I nodded. "I did. In the States."

"Then you know Francesca doesn't let much bother her. She would say, 'it'll be done when it's supposed to be.' You haven't a thing to worry over."

I sighed then pushed my plate away, only crumbs left on the pretty china. "You're right. I'm being overdramatic. It's probably because I've had some trouble sleeping."

"Well then, you must have a glass of wine or two before bed. That's what I do." Cat clinked her Pellegrino against mine. "Now, I overheard Lucia mention the masquerade party to you. You must visit Adriano's shop. He'll fit you for a beautiful gown. But don't tarry too long with finding a gown. Adriano's time is fleeting during events like those."

"I went to his studio with Sergio yesterday. It's incredible. You weren't kidding about how talented he is."

"That's wonderful. I'm so glad you were able to see the shop. Did you find anything?"

"Yes, a gorgeous dress. But that wasn't the one Adriano had in mind. I wasn't feeling well, and we left before I could try on the one stashed away in the back room that he wanted me to wear."

"I'm sure there will be time for that soon enough." Cat's eyes sparkled. "You have to show me when you have it on."

"I will, but I don't know much about the party. Is it open to anyone, or do I need an invitation?"

"You'll need an invitation, but I'm sure Sergio will have one for you."

We chatted for a few more minutes before I had to excuse myself to get back to work, especially since I was to travel with Sergio to Rome that evening. I was excited to about the trip, especially as he'd mentioned it would inspire me for the third panel.

After gathering our dishes, washing them, and putting them away, I stood before the mural and let the beauty of it refuel me. A few more minutes of getting lost in the tangible love between the figure of the romantic couple before me, and I let the world around me fade away while I went to work.

Hours passed, and then little pinpricks of awareness gently eased me from the mural's thrall. I knew who approached and always would. Something connected us, and I was aware whenever he was near. My pulse fluttered in exhilaration, and I took a step back, my gaze still on the painting as strong arms wrapped around my waist. He nuzzled my neck, the spicy scent of him saturating the air around me. I had to stifle the groan that purred up my throat.

"How long until you can be ready?" His deep baritone vibrated along my neck as he continued to trail kisses. When he reached my jawline, I turned in his arms, hungry for more of him.

"Ready?" I arched an eyebrow as laughter spilled from my lips. "I'm ready for you now. Is that what you had in mind?"

"Minx." He nipped at my lips then clearly thought better of it as that spark between us flamed to life. Angling my head, he took my mouth in a toe-curling kiss I never wanted to end.

Putty in his arms, I melted into him, and when he drew back, a whimper at the loss escaped. Our breath mingled as we both fought for control.

"I'm second-guessing taking you to Rome and considering just staying here with you instead."

A sliver of reality returned, as did the reason for our trip. I couldn't give into every desire I had with the man. There was work I needed to get done, and as he'd said before, Rome was where I would find the inspiration needed to complete the final panel. I gifted him a saucy grin. "I'll be ready in ten minutes. Don't go anywhere."

It was safer for him to wait outside for me, something we could both agree on if we were indeed to leave. Unable to resist, I pressed my lips against his one last time before whirling on my heels to get cleaned up and leave with him in record time.

As the door shut behind me, his voice followed. "I'll be waiting." My heart pounded, and giddiness spiraled through me because I realized I'd been waiting my whole life to find him.

SERGIO TOOK me to Rome in his private plane. I was pretty sure the plane came from old family money, but I didn't ask. We visited his home, and afterward, we shopped and shared a few slices of pizza by a crackling fire in a cozy Italian restaurant. The sun had set hours before, and after the second glass of wine, he pulled me from my chair and out the door.

The night was unseasonably warm for late October. We strolled hand in hand along Rome's narrow cobbled streets. "Where are we going?"

He angled his head toward me, a spark of mischief lighting his eyes. "The Trevi Fountain."

"Oh! I've always wanted to visit that." It was said to be so lifelike and magical in its design.

"I think the final scene in the mural should come to you once you see it."

My heart skipped a beat, and excitement buoyed my steps. I didn't doubt him for a second.

"When my brother and I were teenagers, we got it into our heads to jump into the fountain."

I laughed at the image of what he must have been like. "Why would you do that? It's not permitted, right?"

"It's definitely not." He grinned. "But friends dared us, which was all it took. Our parents were furious when they got a call from the officials about what we had done."

Not too far ahead, I made out the lights of the famed Baroque fountain at the base of the Palazzo Poli. Our conversation ceased, and as I was caught up in the wonder of the design, my steps faltered. I'd known what the fountain looked like, but visiting it in person was another experience entirely.

Sergio laughed and pulled me close. It was late, and no one was around. Soft lighting highlighted the lifelike Neptune, sea horses, titans, and the goddess of abundance, to name a few. The mythological beings were set amidst the fluctuating moods of the sea.

Nicola Salvi had designed the most recent model of the fountain, which dated back to the 1700s, but he died before its completion. Giuseppe Pannini saw Salvi's work through by manipulating the marble to curve and dip as if real beings were just under the surface.

We closed the distance, and Sergio's hand shifted to rest on the small of my back. I tilted my head and gazed at his seductive whiskey-colored eyes. If I had been one of his former patients, I doubted that I could've focused on what he was telling me. He wasn't only handsome—he was captivating, patient, innately kind, and generous.

At the edge of the fountain, Sergio moved to stand behind me, resting his chin on the top of my head. His arms wrapped around my waist, and I leaned back. The soothing sound of the water surrounded us, further adding to the tranquil night.

My gaze softened as I relaxed into him. Water splashed, and the trill of a woman's laughter teased the night. I caught a transparent flash of a sodden skirt, there one moment and gone the next. The fountain held history, and through my wine-induced haze, I had been given a romantic glimpse into someone's past as they tiptoed through the water.

"It's beautiful." I was the first to break the spell.

"Not more than you."

Such a charmer.

"Do you know the Trevi Fountain's legend?" His voice vibrated from his chest to my back.

"I do. If we turn our backs to the fountain and toss coins over our left shoulders, our return trip to Rome is guaranteed. I think there's something about health and luck, too, but I can't remember that part. Oh, and there's something attached to throwing in one, two, or three coins, I think."

"Mm, yes. Those are the well-known ones." He bent down and removed his shoes and socks. After rolling up his pants, he urged me to lift my feet, one after the other, slipping my sandals from them.

"What are you doing?"

He grinned at me, lifting the end of my sundress and knotting it just above my knees. "There is another legend that my family swears by."

"Oh really? Wait, we're going in?" I laughed as he lifted me into his arms then stepped over the ledge and into the water. He released my legs, and I slid down the length of his body until my feet were submerged as well. He held out his hand, and I grasped it, allowing him to lead me. "If we get caught..."

"We shouldn't. The officials have left."

My bare feet treaded along the base of the fountain. "Where are the coins?"

"They're gathered each night so they can be used for the needy."

I liked that. He tugged my hand. Water swirled around

my legs as he led me over to the fountain's left side. My eyes widened, taking everything in. The artwork was exquisite, and seeing it up close gave me chills. I skimmed my hand along the sculpted stone, and an answering shiver traveled down my arm. It was magical—every night with him was.

The light touch at my hip drew my attention, and my gaze collided with Sergio's, mesmerizing one. He pulled me close, and my body fit with his, soft against hard. My palms rested on his chest, and I splayed my fingers. As he eliminated the distance between us, I slid my hands up and threaded my fingers in the back of his soft, thick hair. His lips brushed mine, once then twice.

As he caressed my lower lip, I moaned and opened for him. Our tongues tangled, and my pulse kicked up a notch. His strong arms pulled me tightly against him as he deepened the kiss.

My head spun as waves of desire spiked through my blood. Time ceased to exist as we he explored each other's mouths. My body heated, and I lost all sense of where we were.

He pulled back. My fingers touched my swollen lips as our breaths mingled. My legs were weak. He affected me on a level I couldn't explain.

Our surroundings trickled back into my awareness, and I remembered that we stood in the Trevi Fountain. I couldn't explain how he made me feel—it was like a mixture of coming home and overwhelming happiness. The world was still a little fuzzy. My ears buzzed, and I swore I heard Giovanni's voice saying, "I will forever envision you in the arms of the gods."

When one of Sergio's hands left my body, I felt the chill in the air. In the distance, thunder rumbled. Warm air mixed with the cooler nighttime temperature. The fountain emanated a tranquility that even the wafts of gathering fog couldn't dispel.

He clasped my hand and trailed our entwined fingers through the miniature fountain's crossed stream, known as "the small fountain of lovers." As he guided our hands up, his deep voice lured me under his spell. "If lovers drink from the fountain," he said, tracing my lip with his wet finger then slipping past the seam of my lips. I sucked the drops free. He did the same with my hand, licking the drops from my fingers. His other left my back to dip into his pocket. He withdrew a handful of coins and tugged my hand into his full one. We spilled the coins into the water as he said, "The legend says they will always be in love."

CHAPTER 11

Sergio and I spent the night in his home in Rome only to return to Venice the very next day. He didn't have any prior work commitments, and time passed as we talked and enjoyed one another's company both inside and around the Marcello residence. When dinner rolled around, he suggested eating out, and I agreed.

The view from our table at Da Fiore, a quaint Venetian restaurant, overlooked the canal from behind fiery-red window box geraniums. We nibbled on food that was as appealing to the eye as to the palette. I took a sip of my wine while I listened to Sergio talk about his life in Rome. I could have listened to his voice for hours and never tired of him.

"Do you like working on hospital boards?" Ever since he'd first told me, I had been surprised to learn that he'd cut his hours and appointments to serve on hospital boards.

He leaned back in his chair, a faint smile curving his lips. "I love being a surgeon, helping people. I had a driving force to go into the medical profession when I was young—it was almost an obsession. After six years, I realized that being on call and keeping long hours wouldn't be conducive to the family life I wanted. Aunt Francesca was the one who suggested I reduce my schedule and entertain getting involved with the hospital boards. She pointed out that there were other ways to help save people."

"Is she on the hospital board too?" The woman seemed to have a great deal of influence, and I wouldn't have been surprised if her time was spent there as well.

"No. But she did make the suggestion, and it stuck. I have more time and can do consultations if other surgeons request my help. I'm still in the transition process with part of my client base, helping them with a seamless move to another doctor. Being on several boards requires a lot of work—not as many hours as a full-time neurosurgeon, and I've found I enjoy the change."

I grinned. It was his altered hours that allowed him to spend so many evenings with me, and for that, I was grateful. How a month had gone by was beyond me.

"And then I met you." His eyes darkened as he reached for my hand across the table.

I felt the same way. Even though we'd only known each other for a handful of weeks, I couldn't imagine life without him.

"How did you get involved in restorations as an artist?"

How indeed? "I'm not sure how to explain it. Art has been a calling ever since I can remember. When I was in college, I became obsessed with Europe in the early 1900s, the clothing, the occupations, and then the Carnevale di Venezia."

Sergio grinned as he leaned back in his chair.

"I have my masters in conservation, but I love art and doing my own projects on the side. I fell in love with the area, and I painted like a madwoman. I couldn't get enough of the masks, the canals and bridges, the winding streets, and the gondola rides."

"How is it that you never visited Italy before now?"

"My mother had cancer. I didn't want to leave her."

"I'm so sorry, Gianna." He threaded our fingers together then pressed a kiss to the back of my hand. "How is she doing now?"

I took a deep breath and willed the mist from my eyes. "She's in remission and dating someone who loves her very much. They moved in together."

"Now, you don't have to worry as much."

"It makes it easier."

"I interrupted." Sergio leaned on the table, his intense focus trained on me. "Tell me the story of how you came to Venice."

"I was doing quite well, painting and doing restoration work, and then your aunt discovered me. I'd been restoring an impressionistic Renaissance piece that was to travel back to Italy with its owners from their second home in the States. She asked me to visit Venice and restore a mural."

"And the rest is history?"

I nodded and took a sip of my wine.

"You should stay. You belong here."

Just here or with you? It seemed presumptuous to ask.

"My aunt could easily find room for you on the board of the Venice nonprofit for art restoration."

"I would love that."

We chatted for a while about prospects to keep me employed there, which I was all for. There was the alcove mural I longed to restore too. There were a few areas that needed work, including an odd portion that lacked substance around a cinderblock sized section. Working and living in Venice would have been a dream. Sergio promised to talk with Francesca, but I planned to as well, especially since she was to return sometime in November. Our line of conversation piqued my interest in his ancestor, and I asked about Il Verrocchio, whom I knew as Giovanni.

Sergio paused a moment before speaking. "I find myself drawn to many of his old haunts."

A dreamy smile curved my lips. "The Osteria Al Squero?"

"Yes, the canal-side café where we first met. The Trevi Fountain—"

"Oh!" I couldn't help but interrupt him as a glimpse of the woman traipsing through the water came back to me. "Did Il Verrocchio visit there with his girlfriend?"

"Yes, and I'm told the two drank from the miniature lovers' fountain, as we did. After she died and before he took his own life, he swore to search heaven and hell to find her."

I toyed with my napkin and blinked back tears. "So sad."

"Mm." Sergio nodded. "We have several of their notes they left for one another, but we always assumed there would be one more that we just haven't found yet. Did my aunt tell you that after his death, up until about thirty some odd years ago, probably closer to forty, the smell of paint and Venetian plaster permeated the area around the mural on the side of our villa?"

It was so romantic despite the tragedy. "She did. I've wondered why the mural had such minimal damage."

I worried the napkin between my restless fingers. He'd mentioned he was drawn to the places where Giovanni had been, so maybe he would understand the visions and dreams I was having. I couldn't keep it to myself for much longer, and if we were going to further our relationship, then I would have to share with him eventually. *Why not now?*

"You said you were drawn to where Giovanni frequented. Please don't think I'm crazy, but I've seen him before, as well as Sophia."

His head tilted to the side. "In pictures?"

I couldn't stop the grin even if I tried. "That would have been a better explanation, but no. In dreams and visions."

"Tell me." He leaned forward, closing the distance between us despite the table's interference.

I did as he asked. When I finished sharing the scene I'd witnessed while touching the dress in Adriano's studio, understanding lit his amber eyes.

"Now I understand the odd dizzy spells you've been having."

"Yes. I was afraid to tell you about the visions. You don't think something's wrong with me, do you?"

"Of course not. My aunt has similar experiences. And this is Venice. It would be surprising if you didn't experience at the very least a sense of the history while walking through the streets. But if you would prefer, we can run tests and rule out any possible physical causes. However, I don't think we will find anything wrong."

After he assured me once more that he believed me and that nothing between us had changed, I relaxed into an easy conversation with him while we finished our food.

After paying for our meal, he drew me to my feet, and we exited the restaurant onto the street. People strolled hand in hand, several walking with a glass of wine as they shared conversation and laughter. There were no cars, only foot or water traffic. The air was heavy with the scent of fall flowers that grew in abundance from balcony window boxes. Water gently lapped against the nearby canal as a gondola glided by, and climbing vines accented the stunning old-world architecture. It was like taking a step back in time with just the good parts surrounding us.

We crossed a small bridge, stopping in the middle for a mind-numbing kiss. As we separated, his fingers caressed my cheek before linking with mine again. It may have been quick, but there was no doubt in my mind that I'd fallen for him.

We traveled the streets in companionable silence, and my

thoughts wandered back to the mural. The first panel showcased the backs of a man and a woman as they walked hand in hand across a canal by bridge. The second was of the same couple enjoying a gondola ride, their faces in profile only.

I'd begun the sketch I would soon transfer onto wet Venetian plaster for the blank panel and would ask for Sergio's expert eye regarding the design. I wanted it to be perfect before I did the actual work on the mural. The scene would have to be completed in a day before the plaster cured.

Sergio had a gift, as Francesca had claimed, about what Il Verrocchio envisioned for the final panel. Once he explained what he thought it should be, everything had clicked. It was of two lovers kissing by the miniature fountain while standing in the larger Trevi Fountain, exactly what he and I had also done. A chill danced along my spine at the similarities of what had been and what we had reenacted.

As we made our way back to the house, the old-world charm of cafés, churches, and private homes continued to catch my eye. Sergio shared stories of his own or those he'd heard about as he grew up. The city was alive to me in ways I could only have dreamed.

He unlocked the door to the Marcello residence and guided me inside with a hand at the small of my back. "I'll uncork a bottle of red wine. If you want to head out to the landing, I'll bring it out."

I dropped my purse on the island's marble countertop and picked up a discarded cardigan to wear over my blouse and jeans. "Perfect." Most nights Sergio was in Venice, we spent an hour or two in the outdoor nook, relaxing and talking over a glass or two of wine.

When Sergio joined me, I was leaning against the edge of the alcove's watery doorway. The canal was glass-like, and I couldn't help wonder what it was like to grow up surrounded by water. When he pressed the glass of wine into my hand then brushed a kiss to my forehead, I smiled. Mirroring my pose, he wrapped his arm around my waist, gazing out the waterway's door, and took a sip of wine. "What has you so deep in thought?"

I shrugged against him, my mind still wandering. "I was thinking about children. Growing up here, specifically." He turned to me. His brows rose, and I chuckled. "No need to worry. I wasn't thinking about having children."

"Venice is the perfect place to raise kids. Another reason my parents were here so often, besides family and friends, was that my brother and I could run around on our own, and they didn't worry. There is a village to watch out for children here."

"Hmm. Without cars, I'm sure that was one less worry. But the water had to have been a concern."

"Not as much as you would think. Children learn here, just like they do with roads, what's dangerous. I can't even remember an instance of a child falling into the canal and drowning. You'd have to ask Aunt Francesca or Cat, but it's truly a safe environment for kids. Everyone looks out for them."

"There aren't many places to play in the grass, not that it's a big deal."

He tucked a piece of my hair behind my ear. "I'm sure you've seen a group of kids here and there, playing in the campo. The only problem was when we wanted to play football."

"Soccer?" My lips twitched.

He sighed, feigning superiority, but the twinkle in his eyes said otherwise. "Here, we call it football. But imagine playing with a round ball on these cobbled streets."

"Oh." I cringed. "That had to have been a challenge."

"It was, but enjoyable regardless… unless the ball happened to roll into the canal."

I snuggled closer. "Couldn't you go in and get it if you were old enough? Or are there laws about jumping into the canals?"

"There are laws for visitors and adults but leniency where children are concerned. It's not that uncommon to see a kid jumping in to retrieve a ball or off a bridge to cool off. Over the years, canal traffic has increased. But on occasion, you'll see someone doing it."

"So if you weren't able to reach a floating soccer ball, it was considered lost? I can't imagine a group of kids doing that. It had to have been incredibly frustrating."

"Often, there would be a gondola or boat going past that would toss it back to us. It is a wonderful place to grow up, and my brother and I had the best of both worlds with living here and also in Rome." With the hand resting at my hip, he applied gentle pressure and turned me to face him. "Do you want to have kids?"

It was a weighty subject. "I haven't given it a lot of thought, but the more I think about it, I would. Not right now, but someday. Do you?"

"Yes." He took my wine and set both glasses on the table before framing my face in his hands. "Someday."

The touch of his hand at my face drew my attention, tingles following in the wake of his gentle caress. I shifted so I leaned against the wall to focus solely on him. My breath caught in my throat at the naked desire in his gaze. He had the ability to make me feel as if I was the only person in the world who mattered to him. Through our connection, I knew that to be true.

Our gazes locked, and I swore my heart beat in sync with his as he drew me close with infinite care. The heat from his hands stirred a need I didn't think it would be possible to quench. With the first brush of his lips against mine, I sighed into the kiss, molding myself against his body.

He made me forget our surroundings until there was only him. Us. When he was near, all I wanted was to be in his arms. I buried my fingers in his hair, tilting my head for a better angle to deepen the kiss.

When he drew back, I couldn't stop a whimper from escaping, no matter how much I tried. I was tired of taking things only so far. I needed more from him. My hands slid from his hair then down to his shoulders, and I leaned back in his arms.

"I want you, Gianna."

There was no denying how I felt about him. At the brush of his lips across mine, I was lost. I melted against him, falling for him impossibly more. Heat spread from his touch with a breathless intensity. He angled my head to deepen the kiss, sending a volley of shock waves through my system, and my fingers curled into the fabric of his shirt. I never wanted to let him go. Maybe I wouldn't have to.

My mind and body were in complete agreement as he lifted me in his arms and carried me from our grotto and up the three flights of stairs to his floor. Before I knew it, we were in his bedroom. He released me so that my legs slid down his body in slow, tantalizing increments. When my feet were on the floor, he drew back, and I sensed his attempt to slow things down. But that wasn't what I wanted.

I absently took in the chandelier that hung from the ceiling in old-world crystal decadence. The crown molding added to the ambiance, as did the furniture. There was nothing modern about his room, which I loved. And the colors, the deep-red chairs by the floor-to-ceiling windows and the dark end tables and dresser, fit Sergio. At times, I had trouble envisioning either of us in that time period. Surrounded by the furnishings in the room, the décor, it made sense. We made sense.

He tucked a long strand of hair behind my ear, his fingers

trailing down my cheek and resting on the pulse that fluttered at the base. "When I said I wanted you, I didn't mean only for tonight. I meant always."

My breath caught in my throat, and I let go of any concerns about where I would live or what would happen between us because I knew in my heart that we were meant for one another. Always had been. Always would. I nodded, simplifying my response from what I felt engraved in my psyche. "I want the same." We were about to have more than a fleeting experience and I, too, wanted a lifetime of moments with him.

He trailed his thumb over my bottom lip, and a shiver followed in its wake, nerve endings bursting to life. Time stood still, and I lost myself in his touch, in the love shimmering in his passion-filled eyes. We moved toward each other at the same time, and our lips collided in an explosion of desire.

His hands cupped my head, and he angled my face to deepen the kiss while I tugged at his shirt. The need for skin on skin was undeniable. When my fingers grazed his tight abdomen, I felt the quick intake of air from my mouth to his. With deft fingers, our clothes melted away, and once back in his arms, I knew he would show me a world that offered so much more.

When he eased back, the chilly air met my skin, and goose bumps followed in its wake. With a hand at my hip, he backed me up to the bed. "You're so beautiful." I shivered at his sensual tone, my hungry gaze traveling over every inch of him. He lifted me. The duvet was shoved aside, and then I was on my back and cushioned by the mattress, his weight soon to follow. My hair fanned across the pillow, and with unhurried movements, he threaded his fingers through it then trailed them down my arm to take my hand in his. His broad shoulders flexed as he guided my hand so that it was above my head. My fingers twitched in his grasp with the need to explore the well-defined contours my gaze greedily devoured.

Dark promise swam in his eyes. Heat radiated off him as he crowded me, and I wound my leg around his waist, urging him closer. With excruciating slowness, his hand moved up the outer side of my thigh.

I quivered with need as his mouth left my lips to trail kisses along my neck. The scrape of his teeth where my neck met my shoulder sent a dizzying wave of desire, and I gasped. On their own accord, my hands found his shoulders, exploring the contours. Beneath my fingers, the muscles shifted and bulged as he lifted his other hand to cup my nape, angling my head for his kiss. I melted against him as his lips brushed back and forth against mine.

Pings of electricity sizzled through my body with his every caress. Soon, I would be a pile of smoking embers. Leashed strength rippled under my fingertips, and I moaned as he deepened the kiss, his tongue teasing then insistent.

Hypersensitive to his every touch, my body hummed. His length pressed against my thigh, and I arched beneath him. "Sergio. Hurry." I couldn't wait much longer. The buildup of desire from the press of his body boiled to the surface. His gentle caresses changed to urgent, in sync with my escalating need.

When he lifted his head, he tilted mine. I met his burning gaze, which held such promise. "I want you now, Gianna. Tell me you want me too."

I moaned at the image of him doing things to me that I'd only fantasized about. "Yes." My nails dug into his trim waist. He briefly rested his forehead against mine. Like a musician, he controlled my body with every touch, every kiss. As need and want sizzled through me, and I thought I wouldn't be able to last another second from what he was doing, he lifted his lust-filled gaze, and my core exploded with heat, slicking the way for his entry.

My legs shook with anticipation. He pressed against my core, and I pushed back, needing him to fill me. When his fingers traced my seam, I cried out, arching higher to meet him. A sense of urgency chased the feverish nerve pulses, and when he plunged inside, stretching me, I exploded around him in quivering convulsions.

I gripped the bunched-up duvet pushed hastily to the side of the bed with one hand and his arm with the other. His mouth claimed mine in a heated kiss.

My head swam as sensation after sensation crested in waves, following each powerful thrust. His corded muscles flexed and bulged beneath my fingertips. When he slid a hand between our bodies to dip between my folds, teasing the sensitive bundle of nerves there, I cried out, convulsing around him.

He moved from devouring my lips to trailing heated kisses along my neck. He whispered my name, heightening the aftershocks of my orgasm. Then his moan vibrated against my skin, and he chased my climax with his own.

In his embrace, I clung to him for strength, shaken by the sheer height of passion I'd experienced. Our breathing slowly regulated, neither of us willing to move. When he finally pulled out, I felt empty, wanting him all over again.

No words were necessary as he shifted to the side, so his weight no longer covered me, and pulled the duvet over us. His mussed dark hair begged my fingers to run through it, and his brown eyes burned with intense emotion that must have been mirrored in mine. He tugged my body against his. Enveloped in his embrace, I tangled my legs with his.

Moonlight spilled through the window adjacent to the bed. My eyelids grew heavy, and my body relaxed and pressed along his. Content, we dozed.

I woke sometime in the middle of the night to his fingers caressing my cheek as he pushed a few strands of my messy hair back, tucking it behind my ear. A spark of desire stirred to life, and a moan parted my lips. By the look in his hooded gaze, I wasn't the only one that needed to feel what we'd shared again, and with his unhurried touch, I knew each time would feel like the first between us. Every time would. Then his body settled over mine, and I welcomed his weight.

CHAPTER 12

I stirred as the morning sun shone through the windowpane. Snuggling against Sergio in his bed was everything I'd hoped it would be. I swore my soul sighed in contentment, in the rightness of how our bodies fit together. My heart sang from the proximity of him. To me, loving him felt as old as time. It just was. I'd felt it in his touch that first time we'd met, as if that odd tension that had existed all my life had been a taut string, urging me home to Venice.

"Good morning." His deep voice rumbled through his chest and into mine.

Pushing up on an elbow, I grinned. "Good morning to you too."

He pulled me back against him for a lingering kiss.

"You're a bad influence." I drew back, glancing at the bedside clock. Already, it was getting late. It would be difficult to get out of bed. Lying next to him was where I wanted to remain, but there was work to do.

"Mmm, I would say you're the bad influence. I was supposed to stay in Rome the other day, but I couldn't leave your side."

He traveled back and forth too much. I hoped we would be able to figure out a better schedule once I was done with the mural. "How long do you have until you need to leave?"

Eyebrows furrowed, he turned and glanced at the clock. "An hour." At my frown, he took my face and delivered a toe-curling kiss.

My body hummed from his touch, and I slid my hand up his arm to curl around his shoulder. I wanted so much more.

He drew back, breaking the kiss, then chuckled. "Now who's the bad influence?"

"You don't play fair."

He brushed a few strands of my hair from my cheek and tucked it behind my ear, his touch lingering and his eyes darting back to my swollen lips. With a groan, he rolled to his back then sat up, the covers pooling around his waist. "Come on. I'll get some coffee going."

It was hard not to pout because I really wanted to stay in bed with him for a few more hours. But he was right. We both had things to do. Tossing the covers back, I got up.

The bathroom on the third floor was updated with beautiful white marble that had faint veins of gray and a rainfall showerhead. It was heaven, and I had to practically tear myself from the therapeutic experience.

Once I was dressed, I let my nose lead me to where Sergio was by the intoxicating scent of coffee. He flashed me a smile as I walked into the room before turning back to the coffee. "Why don't you leave a few things up here so you don't have to put on the same clothes as yesterday?"

My heart sped up at the loaded question, which clearly indicated we were moving forward with our relationship. "All right. I can bring some up soon." *Did my voice sound breathy?* My cheeks heated at the telltale huskiness. We were moving quickly, but I was more than okay with that. I couldn't get enough of that man.

I took a moment to take him in, leaning my hip against the counter. His dark-mahogany hair was disheveled, and he looked sexily rumpled. He'd thrown on a pair of sweats that rode dangerously low on his hips. I wanted to hook my finger in the waistband and tug.

Then he turned, and I got the full blast of his smoldering expression. My heart sped, and my mouth parted. I knew that look well. His hands found my hips, and he hoisted me onto the counter.

"You can't look at me like that and expect me to ignore it," he said with a growl before his lips came down on mine in a hungry kiss. Within a matter of seconds, he'd peeled off my sweater. I knew the rest of our clothes would soon follow, and my fingers tugged at his waistband with impatience.

It seemed we were both going to be late, but it was totally worth it.

I PUT the last of the paints and tools away for the next time I would work on the mural. An overcast early-evening sky had caused the light to fade, and my ability to work fled with it. I wandered the first floor of the Marcello home with a restless spirit. The spacious and beautiful accommodations were suddenly stifling. Cat hadn't assumed her usual position on her inviting dock that evening, as she had dinner plans with a few of her friends. With Sergio back in Rome for meetings and no sign of Daniela or Adriano, I was left to my own devices. One thing was sure—I couldn't stay inside.

With an oatmeal-colored cable-knit cardigan for warmth, I set out to stroll along Venice's enticing cobbled streets and take in the artistry that had drawn me to the floating city.

Time slipped through my fingers with each passing district. My feet traveled paths that a part of me knew like the back of my hand. Without putting thought into where I was going, trusting in that sense of familiarity that resided deep in me, I soaked up the romanticism and ambiance of the old-world architecture.

A little before dusk, I entered the Cannaregio, the northernmost sestiere, where Sergio and I had had drinks and cicchetti at Al Timon. In the back of my mind, I remembered sitting at Cat's canal-side table, where Adriano, Daniela, and Lucia told me about Antoinette's fresco on her building at the end of the Ponte de Chiodo bridge. The more I revisited the conversation, a destination solidified. I wanted to see her work tonight.

The tourist-free Cannaregio area pulsed with life. A burst of laughter from one of the many restaurants and bars spilled onto the street, infecting me with a joyful vibe. I could imagine the young artist settling, living there. On the anniversary of Adriano's mother's death, I couldn't help but wonder what his life would have been like if she hadn't died.

I paused on one of the many bridges that spanned the canal. Watery refractions shimmered and danced on the building's façade. As dusk trickled in, so did the surrounding homes' and restaurants' twinkling lights. A chill invaded the air, ushering in tendrils of fog, stretching along the rippling canal and obscuring the light's effects on the water. A sense of mystery and romanticism permeated the area, and from my perch midway across the waterway, I scanned the canal for the particular bridge I wished to find.

Not far in the distance, I spotted a bridge without railings. On the faint strains of music and laughter, I neared my destination, hungrily absorbing everything about the ancient bridge and the residence where Adriano's mom, Antoinette, had once lived. Butterflies of excitement and pangs of trepidation fought for supremacy as I stepped onto the short stairs at the start of the structure that would take me across to the front canal-side door. But it was the sight before me that stilled the tumultuous emotions derived from the precarious walkway. Dread clung to my every step as I got closer to the middle, and I shivered as goose bumps formed, not from the cold but in anticipation of something coming.

My eyes adjusted to the dim light of the huddled buildings. Nothing had prepared me for the beauty and skill of the buon fresco. It hovered between life and immortalized movement in the expert application of masterful colors, creating a breathtaking atmosphere that transported me back into the artist's time.

In brilliant hues, two masquerade dancers embraced in a twirl of satin, skill, and concealed demi masks. Yet their identities were unmistakable from a picture Adriano had shown me. Antoinette had captured the emotion in vivid detail on her and Marco's faces and their bodies' movement. Through the arch of her graceful neck and the strain of his arms to hold her to him, the image bled love, longing, and agony in both expression and posture.

The swoosh of a gondola gliding through the water stirred my consciousness while my mind wrestled to separate from the artwork. My surroundings trickled in, though I was reluctant to pay attention. The gentle cadence of the rippling water and voices of the approaching couple that would soon pass under the very bridge where I stood teased my ear with recognition, and I turned, only to pause on Antoinette's transparent form as she came toward me across the bridge.

I should have been shocked, but it wasn't as if it was the first time I'd seen an apparition. From my experiences so far, it seemed there was something I was meant to glean from the visitations.

I observed Antoinette in greater detail. She was clad in a pale formfitting silk dress that contrasted with her olive skin. Her luxurious ebony hair fell over her shoulder in a thick braid. Silver waterfall earrings glistened in the fading light, but her timeless beauty was marred by surprise as she turned to peer into the darkness behind her.

Too many things happened at once, from the small pebble that slid beneath my foot and tumbled off the edge of the bridge to the flash of light to my left to the dark figure shrouded in a hooded cloak that trailed Antoinette's ghostly form.

I wanted to reach out, to warn her. The lone figure trailing her bled ill intent in its hurried steps and clenched fists. A beam of moonlight flared in the diamond on the cloaked person, and by the dainty hand and lock of dark shoulder-length hair that had escaped the hood, I had a good guess of who it was.

Words were said, but I could not hear them and was not part of the glimpse into the past that Antoinette's spirit showed me. The agitation then worry that clouded her features told me she knew who trailed her every step as she tried to brush her off and put distance between them.

I attempted to move once again, but my body was locked down, my muscles refusing to obey as the projection of Antoinette and the woman chasing her closed the distance on the bridge.

In a recess of my mind, I registered that the gondola's progression halted on the water below where I was. The two passengers pierced my haze in recognition, and I gasped as Adriano jerked from David's embrace, sitting up straight. As he called my name, the alarm in his voice sent zaps of shock through my system.

I stood precariously on the edge of the bridge. Every muscle in my body went taut as Antoinette's expressive eyes widened in terror. The cloaked figure raised an arm, hand fisted around a rock, then struck Antoinette. There was a sickening crack upon impact as the object struck her head. Her body jerked, shoved from the side by an unidentifiable force of impact. She reached for me in a desperate attempt to halt her fall as blood bloomed on her forehead, her gaze unfocused.

I teetered at the edge, Adriano and David's frantic pleas mixing with Antoinette's horrified scream as she tumbled from the bridge. In a rippling swirl of silk, her body sunk into the murky depth.

The image of Antoinette's still form striking the water hadn't affected Adriano and David's gondola as the scene unfolding layered over where they were. I could only assume that the ghostly vision had transposed over the exact spot where they were.

Time stood still. The horror of what I'd witnessed shackled me with one foot firmly in the veil of the past. Locked in place, my body strained from following her descent. I lost track of my surroundings, of the passage of time in the present, only focusing on the air sawing in and out of my lungs as I tried to make sense of the crime I'd witnessed.

Strong arms wrapped around me. I was lifted from the walkway and tugged back. The ache in the top of my feet told me that I'd been perched on the very edge on my toes, millimeters from plunging into the canal along with Antoinette.

"What were you thinking? You could have fallen in." Adriano's shaken features swam into focus as I separated myself from the past. My fingers threaded through his long thin braids as I gripped his shoulder. David hovered at my side, and I realized we were standing at the end of the bridge, no longer suspended over the waterway.

Moored to the side walkway about a foot from the bridge, their gondolier waited. I blinked the world into sharper focus. Concern etched lines around Adriano's mouth, and his question snapped me back into clarity. I gripped one of his hands tightly. "Did you see her?"

"Who?" Wariness tinged his brown eyes to a deeper shade.

My gaze flicked over my shoulder at the fresco then back at Adriano. "Antoinette."

A tremor ran through his arms, and his fingers flexed on my back. "You saw my mother? Her ghost?"

Oh no. Tears filled my eyes at the mixture of hope and pain that consumed him. David pulled Adriano to his side, offering support while the two waited for my response. All I could do was nod. I wasn't sure it was right to tell him. "Maybe I was mistaken?" I wasn't, but I couldn't tell what was best, the truth or perhaps a partial omission.

Adriano leaned into David, his gaze ping-ponging from me to the fresco that no doubt haunted his existence. I couldn't imagine. The image of his parents lovingly preserved before him had to offer a mixture of comfort and longing for what couldn't be.

"Let's all go get a drink." David patted his arm then went to pay the gondolier, cutting their ride short. Back at our side, he urged us to move away from the bridge and the fresco. "We can go to Al Timon."

The fog had thickened, no longer fingers tiptoeing through the canals and cobbled streets but murky tufts of obscurity. The floating city, steeped in history, called to my soul. It was as if I walked on a tightrope, hand in hand with lives past and present. The steady presence of Adriano and David helped to ground me as we wove through busy tables at the restaurant to find a small one tucked in the corner beneath twinkling lights and inches from the edge of the canal.

Silence stretched between our shell-shocked trio. None of us spoke until after we placed our order and received our grappa, followed by spritzers. Adriano lifted his head, his fragile vulnerability shimmering on the surface of his beautiful face. "Tell me everything."

But I couldn't. I wouldn't do anything to hurt the talented man hanging on the vivid details I would describe to him.

Instead, I shared that what I saw had not been the result of a suicide but left out how she'd looked before slipping, as she'd hurried across the bridge on a fog-filled night, leaving out the dark figure that trailed then attacked his mother. It would only have invoked a sense of unresolved pain and despair for her final moments.

"I wish I'd seen her." Adriano's voice was heavy with regret, and David wrapped an arm around his shoulders, drawing him close.

I almost wish I hadn't. The dark figure behind Antoinette haunted me.

"Maybe someday you will, but at least we know she was there." David rubbed a hand up and down Adriano's arm, offering comfort. With his free hand, he signaled to our waiter for a refill. "And that it was a tragedy, not self-inflicted."

I hated seeing Adriano down, the ache for Antoinette's missing presence a stark pain in his usually warm brown eyes. I squeezed his hand as the waiter stopped by our table, clearing empties and replacing them with another shot of grappa and round of drinks.

"Do you have any stories from when you were little? Maybe talking about her would help. At the very least, it would be a good way to remember her on the anniversary of her death."

A half smile curved Adriano's mouth, and his gaze grew distant. "I don't have a lot of memories because she died when I was five years old, but I remember her laughter. And how she hugged. It was with her whole heart and was the best feeling."

Her mural flashed in my mind. I could easily picture his mom being that way. Her painting was so alive. Seeing it had been an almost tangible experience.

"Cat has shared stories about her, and I get a hazy memory of some of them." Adriano took a sip of his drink then leaned back into David's side. "She used to make Christmas cards, something I remember doing with her before she died. It was a big production. She would make hot cocoa, put on music, and then we would each sketch several pictures for the front of the card. Well, mine were potato-head figures and scribbles. When we were done, she'd lay them out on the kitchen table."

"I love that." I rested my elbow on the table, the palm of my hand supporting my chin.

"Mmm," David murmured, echoing my sentiments.

"Mom's drawings were always amazing, so intricate and… lifelike. She exuded energy, and it was impossible not to be happy around her." He shrugged his shoulders, a small laugh escaping his lips. "I did not inherit her talent."

"What?" David's eyes went wide, the pale green flashing as he turned to Adriano. "You can sketch anything. We have hundreds of your designs, several that I insisted on framing. Do not sell yourself short."

Red stained Adriano's cheeks as laughter from boisterous young adults from one of the moored and converted gondolas traveled through the still-packed outdoor area. "Well, at five, my artistic ability was age-appropriate. But it didn't matter to her. I would always choose one that she drew. How could I not? She wouldn't hear of it. She would pick one of mine and make a fuss about how much she loved it, and there was no other that could grace our Christmas card."

"She sounds wonderful." My heart swelled at his story. "How did you make the cards?"

"We would carve the design on a lino block then roll ink on with a brayer. Once it was coated in ink, we would put the front of the card facedown and roll a clean brayer over the paper. That part was easy. The carving took longer." Adriano and David shared a look. "I don't remember doing it more than twice as I was young, but it left a lasting impression, and I have all the cards we made together when I was little. She always saved one and put it in a scrapbook. It's something my dad continued with Daniela and me, and David and I also adopted the tradition."

I wanted to ask if Lucia took part in making the cards, but it didn't feel right to insert his stepmom as Adriano remembered Antoinette. It seemed the two women were opposite in demeanor.

My phone pinged, and I pulled it out of my pocket. The *I miss you* text from Sergio sent heat to my cheeks. I replied back that I missed him, too, and that I was out with the guys.

When he texted, *Sleep in my bed tonight, I want to imagine you there, even if I can't physically hold you tonight,* I almost moaned out loud.

"What was that?" David leaned forward his smile wide.

"What?" My cheeks were hotter, and I knew I was furiously blushing.

"Uh-uh." Adriano shook his head, his finger circling in the air, encompassing my face. "You can't blush like that and tell us it was nothing."

I laughed then shook my head in exasperation. "You two are impossible." My heart swelled at how cute they were. "It was Sergio."

"Thought so." David sing-songed. "Tell us everything."

"Nope." I wasn't going there. "Tonight is about memories and friendship, not my love life."

"Oh!" Adriano pointed at me. "I knew it. They're serious."

"Stop," I begged, dissolving into a fit of giggles.

"All right. We'll be merciful on you tonight. But not next time." David winked then turned his attention back to Adriano. "Speaking of memories, tell Gianna how you used to dress." Then he laughed at Adriano's eye roll.

Adriano lifted his grappa shot, and we did the same after clinking the glass edges before taking sips. Adriano huffed out a sigh. "Seems I was dramatic even at a young age."

"That's not what I meant." David chuckled.

"Tell me." Warmth settled in my stomach from the grappa, and I couldn't help the happiness spiraling through me from being in their company. Adriano thought the charismatic gene stopped with his mother, but he was wrong. It was very much alive in him.

"From what Marco told me, when I was very young, I had this red cape that I would wear every day, no matter where we were going."

"He still has it. It's adorable," David added.

"I wore it so much that it frayed at the ends. Mom sewed a strip of purple at the bottom. From what I'm told, I insisted on the color rather than the matching red. Once, someone commented about how I shouldn't wear it to mass. Dad told me that Mom went to mass the next week with me, both of us wearing capes."

"Oh, I love her." Antoinette sounded amazing.

"Mm-hm," David agreed. "The next time for mass, Marco joined them, also wearing a cape." He caught my eye and the silent O my mouth had formed. "It was a different church than he regularly attended."

Lucia had to have known. But by that point in their affair,

from what Sergio had told me, they were already estranged and he'd wished to end their marriage.

I shook my head at how well Antoinette and Marco had fit together, saddened by the way her life was cut short, forever changing both Adriano's and Marco's. Sensing Adriano needed a change of subject, at least for a little while, I asked them how they met. David started the story, while Adriano interrupted, calling him out on details omitted. My cheeks ached from smiling so widely for so long.

I spent the remainder of the evening with both of them as Adriano reminisced about what he could remember and what his father, Marco, told him to keep his mother alive for the son they shared. A shocking sighting shifted to a cherished night where we toasted to Antoinette's life, regardless of how it was cut short.

As the clouds parted, stars filled the inky sky, and we stood after settling our bill. Rather than stumble the twenty-plus minutes home, we climbed into one of the waiting gondolas to carry us to the house and bring our evening full circle. But I couldn't shake the two brushes I'd had with succumbing to the arms of the canal and how restless spirits sought to lure me from the living to their side.

CHAPTER 13

Adriano and David made sure that I got safely back to the Marcello home. After hugs goodnight, I stumbled inside and locked the door behind me. Exhaustion beat at me, and all I wanted to do was to fall into bed and black out.

I leaned against the doorframe that led to the balcony off the bedroom and clutched my cardigan tightly. The effects of drinks with Adriano and David had worn off. It was late, but I couldn't sleep. I'd gotten used to Sergio lying beside me. I felt his loss deep in my psyche, as if he wouldn't be coming back. It was ridiculous, and logically, I understood that. But some part of me feared the heartbreak of separation.

It was strange, all the things that had happened to me since coming to Venice. The more they did, the easier they were to accept. But it had never happened to me back in the States, other than a little déjà vu here and there.

Fifteen minutes later, face and teeth scrubbed and pajamas on, I lay on the inviting mattress with the fluffy white duvet chasing away the chill of the room. Sleep was slow to come, and I tossed and turned, the image of the ghostly Antoinette and the figure behind her disturbing me on a level that, when I was on the cusp of slumber, followed me.

I couldn't fully exorcise seeing Antoinette's murder from my thoughts. Antoinette's frightened face flashed over and over, her half-Italian and half-French words a jumble that my brain couldn't piece together. But the fear and despair in her tone and the way they'd rearranged her features from serene and breathtaking to taut and terrified did. Shadows and fog engulfed the pursuing figure, and it was impossible to glimpse a face. But one thing I was sure of—it had been a woman.

I hadn't wanted to confide in Adriano or David about what I'd witnessed, but I couldn't keep it to myself. After a glance at the late hour, I almost didn't call him. But I needed to hear his voice, and that overrode any concern.

It only rang twice before he picked up on his end with a groggy "ciao." As soon as I apologized for waking him, the sleepiness had cleared from his deep tones, and I had his full attention.

His voice deepened. "I'm glad you called."

"I couldn't sleep and just needed to hear your voice."

"Mmm. I wish I was lying next to you. There is something I could do to tire you out."

"I would love that." A husky laugh slipped past my lips, and I couldn't help the grin from forming. Calling him had been the right thing to do. Already, I felt lighter even without telling him the real reason behind needing to hear his voice. I would share everything with him, just not over the phone.

"You're the one I've been waiting for all my life, Gianna."

I snuggled under the covers, inhaling his scent on the pillow beside me, comforted by both that and his voice. We chatted for a few more minutes, which helped me take my mind off the night's events. As the minutes ticked by, my yawns increased in frequency. After I'd assured him again that I was all right, we said good night.

I kept the phone close as my eyes drifted shut, a smile curving my lips. Deep down, I felt that unbreakable connection that Sergio had referenced. It was only getting stronger with the more time we spent together. And even with the visions and dreams, I wouldn't change my coming to Venice for anything in the world.

Moonlight spilled into the room, and my gaze lazily followed its silvery beam until the mask we'd made together on Sergio's nightstand caught my focus. It became the catalyst that hurtled me into another entanglement with Sophia. I tried to fight it, as I didn't think I could take much more that night, but she was insistent. After a short struggle, I gave in because I knew there would be a reason—or a warning—that she had to show me.

The room Sergio and I shared morphed into the crowded streets the night of the masquerade. I walked once more in Sophia's body as she traveled amidst a horde of masked people wearing lavish gowns, dapper suits, and full or demi masks. *The quaint Venice streets overflowed with mascaraed partiers reveling in the potentially sinful event's inconspicuousness. Excitement and a trickle of expectation hung in the air as I wove through the people searching for the only one that mattered —Giovanni.*

The crimson satin and black lace of my gown swirled around my feet. Black gloves covered my arms from the tips of my fingers to my elbows, and the demi mask hid my identity. But my Giovanni knew what I was wearing and would be searching for me as well. He, too, only wore a demi-mask, but his was all black, unlike my two-toned one. My heart thundered against my chest as

I wove through the rush of happy partygoers. I couldn't wait to feel his arms around me. Amid the masquerade, anonymity would keep us safe. I didn't think anyone would recognize me.

To dance in his arms in the open was a dream we both shared. The day before, as we strolled together on the Lido shores, we'd come to the mutual decision that we couldn't deny a love like ours. We completed each other. If only there was a way to break off my engagement without shame befalling my family. I'd fought the inevitable for too many sleepless nights. No longer. My family and Edoardo's would never accept my desertion. The only chance was if we ran away together, something that I hoped Giovanni would agree to. It was what I planned to talk with him about tonight.

I never wanted to go back. It would be the last night I would spend under Edoardo's family's roof. No matter the sacrifices, Giovanni was worth them all.

I bounced off an overzealous couple who attempted to twirl to the music. Brushing off drunken apologies, I pressed on. We were to meet in Piazza San Marco. Anticipation drew me forward, and the intense love we shared shielded me from the reckless souls that continued to hinder my progress.

My love was very tall, and I knew I would spot him first. Another sweep of the people in my immediate vicinity didn't result in the one I sought. Ruthlessly, I pushed aside the first stirrings of unease. The hairs along the back of my neck rose, and I cast a wary glance behind me. When no one stood out in the sea of colorful gowns and masks, I took a steadying breath before squeezing past a portly man whose belly laugh brought a smile to my lips.

There! With that deliciously handsome square jaw and broad shoulders and a head taller than most was my Giovanni. His black hair matched his demi mask and dark suit. Intimidation and prowess bled from his form. There was no mistaking my love for anyone else. Shorter than those around me, I rose onto my tiptoes, my arm stretched overhead as I waved in an attempt to attract his attention.

Frustration beat at me. We were so close, I could almost feel what it would be like in his arms, and I wanted that desperately. In his embrace, I was home. Complete. I would do anything for him, even give up the prestigious life my family had negotiated. Nothing mattered but living every day, basking in the magnificence of his love.

His dark-gray eyes scanned the crowd, and the moment he spotted my hand, my heart soared. There were several feet and many people between us, but he would find me. He promised he always would.

As I moved forward, a hand wrapped around my arm in a vise-like grip. My body jerked back, no longer obeying me but the one who shackled me. The swarm of people swallowed me from sight, and the distance from reaching Giovanni expanded exponentially. In a wash of fear, my limbs weakened, and I panted at all I would lose because I knew who restrained me without turning—Edoardo.

I gasped and jackknifed awake, desperate to escape the pain, despair, and devastation that flooded every cell of Sophia's—my—body. In the morning's twilight, I struggled to stave off the crushing terror of the inevitable outcome of Edoardo's discovery. Fat tears rolled down my cheeks as I frantically cataloged every piece of antique furniture in the room through watery eyes, needing to ground myself in the reality that I was safe and no longer trapped in his grasp.

As the familiar items in the room dispelled the nightmares and the past dissipated to where it belonged, I couldn't shake the overwhelming anguish of being caught by Edoardo.

The intense emotions from both dreams and visions of Antoinette and Sophia faded from my battered mind, and for a while, my limbs relaxed into the pillow-top mattress. I wished with every fiber of my being that Sergio was there and I was safe in his embrace, firmly rooted in the present and the rightness of our connection.

Seconds turned into minutes, and I breathed easier, sinking into the blissful blackness of a deep, dreamless sleep until the bright rays of the morning pulled me into the new day.

CHAPTER 14

My hands curled around the coffee cup, and I stifled a yawn. My fingers trailed over the back of the couch, which beckoned me to lie down for a few more minutes. *Why is it so hard to wake up this morning?*

A puff of air pushed past my lips as I revisited the visions from the night before. Sophia was like a wisp of smoke to me, the shape of her dissipating and difficult to recall, as if it truly had been only a dream, even if I was awake while experiencing it. In the aftermath of my experience with Antoinette's ghost and what had really happened to her that fateful night, I felt as though I walked on shaky ground.

I went through the motions of getting ready for the day, starting the coffee then getting dressed. It wasn't long until the heavenly rich scent of coffee filled the first floor, and I poured myself a cup then opened the door to seek out Cat. There was a chill in the air, and I shivered, thankful for the warm drink in my hand. Like clockwork, Cat was settled at her outdoor table, and I quickened my pace to her side.

At my approach, she turned and met my gaze, a brilliant smile spreading across her face and lighting her eyes.

"Mind if I join you?"

"Ah, Bella. You are always welcome."

Undisturbed and still, the canal was a canvas for the surrounding homes. Vivid colors and old-world architecture cast watery images, enhancing Venice's magic, something I felt in my blood more often than not.

Cat cleared her throat, and I forced myself to get out of my head and visit with her. "It's a beautiful morning. I debated making breakfast here or going to San Marco for brioche."

A croissant sounded good.

"I miss eating there. It's something Lorenzo and I used to do." She waved away the words. "But you know all about that. My good friend Maribel and I are going to stroll to Millevini this afternoon for a wine tasting and to restock."

"That sounds like fun." I took a sip of coffee, savoring the warmth as it spread through me before diving into a subject that I was having trouble letting go of. "Cat, did you know Antoinette well?"

A faraway haze coated Cat's tired eyes before she turned to glance at the Dellucci home, where Lucia had just stepped out onto the second-floor balcony. Marco was already seated with a cup of coffee and newspaper in hand. "I had the pleasure of being a friend. She had a vibrant personality. It was impossible not to gravitate toward her."

"Like Adriano?"

She shifted her focus back to me. "Yes, very much so. There are some people who just exude creativity and talent. Their personalities draw others in. What is that saying? Like a butterfly to a flame?"

I grinned. It was prettier that way, but no. "Like a moth."

"Well, in theory, that's how it was with Antoinette. Marco was deeply in love with her. It didn't take much. When she first came to Venice with the driving need to soak up the floating city, to paint her masterpiece, all it took was for her to walk by him, and he was lost."

"Adriano has some memories of her, but he was only five when she passed, so it isn't a lot." I paused to study Lucia from a distance, unsure of what I wanted to know. "I just wonder how someone like that…"

Cat patted my hand. "It's one of life's many mysteries. But one day, maybe you will know. When you pass through the veil to the other side, you can ask Antoinette yourself."

"Perhaps." Or maybe I knew enough already.

"*Ciao, belle signore.*" Sergio's deep baritone made a shiver of delight roll over my body.

"Hello to you too." I turned my face up to accept his light kiss. "I didn't expect you back so soon."

The twinkle in Cat's eyes elicited a laugh from me. I, too, was lost at the first sight of Sergio, as had been Marco to Antoinette. Funny how such things happened.

"If you don't mind, Cat, I have plans for Gianna."

I turned in my seat so that I was facing him. "Oh? What might those be?"

"Pff. Do not ruin a perfectly good surprise, Bella. Go." Cat waved us away. "Enjoy your time together."

Sergio grasped my hands and drew me to my feet, and when I was standing by his side, he addressed Cat. "We'll bring you a surprise tomorrow."

"Off with you two, then. I'm already anticipating what my gift will be." Cat winked then tugged her shawl tighter around her shoulders as a chilly breeze danced through the canal, stirring strands of her long silver hair.

I gave Cat's shoulder a gentle squeeze then looped my arm through Sergio's before he led me to the house. After rinsing my coffee cup, I grabbed my purse. "Where are we going?"

A grin curved his lips, and that mischievous glint I was

addicted to brightened his brown eyes to a beguiling whiskey color. "You'll have to wait and see."

My fingers curled around the strap of my purse, and I worried about the casual jeans and T-shirt I wore, paired with one of my favorite cardigans. "Am I dressed okay?"

He intertwined our fingers then tugged me close. Tucking a strand of my hair behind my ear, he leaned in and whispered, "You're beautiful." With infinite gentleness, his lips brushed across mine, leaving dizzying tingles in its wake. "And you're dressed perfectly. Perhaps bring a scarf for your hair, as it's windy where we are going, and a change of clothes. We're staying overnight."

"Where?" When he released me from his arms, the electricity of his touch remained.

His laugh filled me with warmth inside, and I couldn't help but grin. "If I told you, it wouldn't be a surprise."

With a roll of my eyes, I grabbed a silk scarf and hair tie then packed an overnight bag, and we were off. We took a water taxi then boarded his jet at Venice's Marco Polo Airport. In a whirlwind of flying, disembarking, then Sergio whisking me into a waiting car, we finally arrived at our destination.

Not far off the Amalfi Coast, we wove through winding roads to a family-owned vineyard boasting hundred-year-old vines. Sergio clasped my hand as we walked through lush green vines, which hugged the rolling hills with the Alpine mountains a backdrop in the distance. It was also something I could picture us returning to do again throughout the years. "Is this allowed?" There was something magical about walking through the rows of vines, and I couldn't help but fall in love with the romanticism of the area and Sergio's planning of our excursion.

"The vineyard has tours, but I know the owner and

obtained permission. We could walk for a while then have a wine tasting and lunch."

"It's beautiful here. Thank you for arranging this."

"It is." He tugged on my hand until I stopped and faced him. "But not more beautiful than you."

He tucked a few strands of hair behind my ear, and a shiver followed in the wake of the pads of his fingers. I lost myself in the love shining from his brown eyes. Even if I had wanted to turn away, which I didn't, I couldn't have. As he lowered his head, our lips inches apart, my heart rate sped.

The sensation of his lips against mine was something I didn't think I would ever tire of. There was a heady combination of completion, as if we'd done so a million times before, and exhilarating newness, as if it was the first. No one had ever made me feel the way Sergio did.

When he drew back, we were both slightly out of breath. His hand trailed down my arm until our hands clasped. Passion smoldered in his gaze, and I wanted to pick right back up where we were, but it seemed we had other plans.

"Come. Our lunch and wine tasting are waiting, and I want you to meet Maximo and Sarah."

We resumed walking. "How do you know them?"

"Sarah was a patient of mine, and through her, I met her husband, Maximo."

Through the rows of vines, I spotted a house at the bottom of the hill. After another fifteen minutes, we arrived. The front door opened, and a woman stepped out. My fingers twitched against Sergio's, and he gave my hand a reassuring squeeze. I don't know why I was nervous—maybe because I hadn't been invited to the home of friends of his before. It felt like a big deal.

When she approached, I wanted to check my nails for paint and tuck my hair into a neat bun. I guessed she was twenty years my senior but possessed a warmth that made my smile just as genuine as hers. A small beauty mark resided on the corner of her upper lip. Her sleek dark hair fell just above her shoulders, and a few wispy bangs added youth to her features and reflected in the sparkle in her hazel eyes.

After introductions, she looped her arm in mine and pulled me with her. "Come. Maximo has our lunch set up in the garden."

About the same height, I easily matched her stride. But when we rounded the back end of the house, I came to a standstill at the sight before us. It was breathtaking. The wild abandon to the flowers appealed to me. A tall thin man stood by the table, a bottle of wine in hand. With thinning hair and bushy eyebrows, laugh lines around his eyes and mouth, he waved us over.

Sergio made introductions. He pulled my chair out for me, and I sat at a table overflowing with mouthwatering scents of food. There were several wineglasses at the head of the table where Maximo had four bottles of wine.

Sarah was across me and passed food around the table. Once we each had helpings of rustic, rich pasta with robiola and truffles, Maximo poured a small amount of red wine into glasses then handed them out. We tasted wines, sampling them with food, and I found my favorite Nebbiolo to compliment the meal. The century-old grapes offered red fruit and a rose aroma. The wine swirled over my palate with grippy tannins, and a triage of fruit, spice, and earthy flavors followed in its wake.

When the food had a serious dent in it, I leaned back in my chair, Sergio's arm draped around my shoulder, warding off the slight chill in the air.

"Sergio mentioned you're from the United States. Tell us a little about yourself, Gianna," Sarah prompted. Elbow on the table, she rested her chin on her hand, giving me her undivided attention.

I took a sip of wine, wondering what I should talk about. Art seemed the easiest. "My mom is an artist, watercolors mostly. I grew up working beside her from a young age. I had my own easel in the studio, and while she would paint, so would I. It was something we did every day, and it stuck." Sergio traced circles on my arm as I talked, and I tucked myself closer to his side despite the chair's restrictions. "Those are some of the best memories I have with her."

"Has she passed away?" Maximo's eyebrows furrowed.

"No." I laughed at the way I'd told the story. "I have no idea why I said it like that. Fortunately, she's well and lives in a thriving art community. I don't see her as often as I would like. I guess that's where I was going with that. She's from Tuscany, originally."

"And your father as well?" Maximo topped off Sarah's wine before doing the same for me.

"My father is Italian-American. While my father's business is based in the States, he had a meeting in Switzerland. My mother happened to be vacationing with friends at the same ski lodge where my dad was staying. My parents met and fell in love there. Anyway, that's where my interest in art came from… and my Italian heritage."

"Artistry runs in both our families' histories," Sergio shared. "Did you know that Gianna is restoring and finishing the mural on the side of our family home in Venice?"

We talked and laughed for another two hours before Sergio and I took our leave, but not before purchasing a few bottles of wine as a gift for Cat.

Back in the car, he drove along the winding roads toward the coast. It was getting close to sunset, and I stifled a yawn from the enjoyable but long afternoon.

Sergio drove with one hand, his other playing with my

fingers, which rested on the console between us. We were always touching in some way. I found the need for contact with him almost as natural as breathing. He'd become an integral part of me almost since the moment we'd met.

As we traveled down the hillside, the sparkling blue of the Amalfi Coast held me captive with its inviting beauty. It wasn't until he parked at a quaint bed-and-breakfast that he shared his next surprise.

"We stayed longer at Maximo and Sarah's than I thought we would. We have one more excursion tonight after a quick dinner." He flashed the sexy grin that made my knees weak. "A sunset sail along the coast."

Not quite hungry and with a half hour before we had reservations at a beachside restaurant along the coast, we strolled the beach and worked up an appetite. When it was time to go to the restaurant, we were seated at a table secluded from the rest and with a beautiful view of the sea. We ordered salads, both of us opting for something light.

Across from me, I met Sergio's watchful gaze, no doubt picking up on my exhaustion. "I'm glad we're spending the night."

He paused, his fork halfway to his mouth. "Is everything all right?"

With a shrug, I moved a few of the tomatoes to the side of my salad. "I didn't sleep all that well. Last night, I went to see Antoinette's fresco on her former residence."

His fork clattered to his plate. "On the eve of her death?"

"Apparently." I grimaced at the sheer absurdity of my actions in a city where the past and present walked hand in hand. I rolled the napkin between my fingers in my lap as I debated whether to tell him what I couldn't share with Adriano.

After a deep breath, I dove in, sharing with Sergio what I was afraid to verbalize out loud, lest he think I was crazy.

But Adriano and David hadn't, and maybe he would have an open mind or an explanation about what was happening and why it seemed that ghosts from the past kept haunting me.

Sergio covered my hand with his much larger one, the warmth of his touch holding the chill of the experience at bay. With the simple gesture, I made my decision.

The first words came haltingly then the entire story poured from me about how I'd witnessed Antoinette being struck by the stranger then plummeting into the canal. He dragged his chair around to my side of the table and drew me into his arms as I summed up where I had been and the vision of Antoinette and the cloaked figure that attacked her, ending with Adriano and David pulling me from the dangerous edge of the bridge.

"Are you okay?"

I heard the worry that laced his voice and hoped with everything in me that he wouldn't suggest I needed to see a psychiatrist. "For the most part, yes." But after what Sophia had shown me in Adriano's shop, and Sergio's acceptance then, too, it made it easier to confide in him. But there was still lingering doubt. I closed my eyes, deciding to go for it, to ask him outright what he thought. "Do you believe me, or do you think I'm losing my mind?"

"As a doctor, I would suggest tests to rule out possible causes. But as a Venetian, I'm no stranger to seeing the past invading the present. And then there's Aunt Francesca, growing up and witnessing her premonitions come to light, as we discussed before. Of course, I believe you. Have faith in me to be there for you."

A rush of air pushed past my lips as I expelled a deep breath.

"I'm sorry you had to experience that alone. I wish I had been there for you when this happened."

"I know." I clutched the napkin tightly between my fingers.

"So, the reason you didn't tell Adriano and David about the cloaked figure?"

"For one, I would have no proof, and it would cause so much pain for Adriano to know someone murdered his mother as opposed to an accident."

"That's true. But there's something else. I can see it in your expression."

I sat on the edge of my chair, leaning toward him. "I have a suspicion about who the other person was. There was a flash of a large diamond on her hand. I didn't get a clear look, as it was fairly dark. But in the moonlight, it appeared to be the same one Lucia wears."

There was a moment of silence, and I shivered in anticipation over how he would react. There were many times when his voice would change from inviting to guarded around Lucia. I hoped that he would stay open-minded.

"That is a problem." Sergio sighed. "Even if we were able to find the cloak, there would be no evidence against her. People in the area were interviewed the night of Antoinette's death. Surprisingly, no one saw it happen. And telling Adriano... I would have to agree that no good would come of it."

I let my eyelids momentarily drift closed as Sergio lifted the burden and shared the weight of it all. Talking to him had been the right thing to do.

"Lucia raised him." I couldn't even process it fully. "She might not be a warm and inviting person, but she took him in. I can't imagine the betrayal he would experience in knowing that his stepmother murdered his real mom."

He drew me against him, and I released my tenacious grip on the worried napkin. As his fingers combed through my hair, I released the pain and worry of the experience into our shared embrace. The last of my tears dried. With a gentle swipe of his thumbs, he wiped the trails away from my cheeks and tilted my face to meet his in a drugging kiss. Any thoughts I had fled in the wake of his tongue dancing with mine. My fingers threaded through his silky hair, and I tugged him closer.

By the time we parted, we were both out of breath and overheated. He kneaded the back of my neck, further easing the tension that resided there. "Have you spoken with Adriano since last night?"

"No." My voice was whisper soft. "I didn't tell him about the other person, only that Antoinette slipped. And that she hadn't taken her own life."

"You did the right thing, Gianna." He touched his forehead to mine.

"I know." But I couldn't help the need to scream over the injustice of how her life was taken, robbing Adriano of his mother. "But what if it really was Lucia? The ring…"

Fury burned in Sergio's eyes. "That woman causes all my instincts to flare. I don't doubt that you're right. But"—he shook his head, frustration evident in the slow movement —"without any physical proof, there isn't much we can do."

I tugged his plate from across the table so it was in front of him, wanting him to remain close.

By mutual agreement, we moved on to other topics, as I no longer wanted to revisit my experiences from the night before. Our time in the restaurant came to an end, as we both wanted to keep the appointment he'd made to go on the sunset sail.

I didn't think much could top the day, but I was wrong. Sailing off into the sunset in his arms then a romantic night together at a bed and breakfast… I wasn't sure if he knew it yet, but I was never letting him go.

A few days had passed since Sergio and I had returned from our bed-and-breakfast surprise trip. I'd had coffee with Cat the following morning in an attempt to reenergize my sagging mind and body. The spirited older woman had entertained me with tales of her younger days with her husband and the adventures they'd had. After a while, my pulse had kicked up to semi-alive, and she described how they'd taken an idea for their floral business and grown it into the success it still was, enabling her to live in comfort while others ran it for her. Her story was inspiring.

A part of me was envious of the incredible partner who'd loved her enough to fill their remaining years together with happy memories until they were reunited one day. But I, too, adored and wished her an eternity of timeless romance. Sergio's handsome face swam in my mind, and I wanted a similar outcome over many years with him. I thought it was probable. I'd never felt so connected to a man, so enthralled and possibly obsessed.

The day flew by in a blur of activity as I began work on the final scene sketches for the fresco, as the cleaning of the mural was complete. Francesca had been correct—the very person who helped me envision what Il Verroccio would have done had taken me to the Trevi fountain and shown me. And in an hour, I would be meeting him for dinner.

After cleaning up and putting everything away, I took a quick shower and was ready when Sergio rang the bell. I couldn't help the jolt of pleasure at how sweet he was to arrive at the door like it was an actual date and we didn't already live in the same building. He was very respectful and gallant, even though I was more than ready for him to take advantage of our living arrangements much more than we already had.

With barely contained excitement to see him, I opened the door. Sergio stood before me in a white button-down shirt and dark-gray pants, holding a bouquet of flowers, and I was glad I'd chosen the long maxi skirt and fitted black top. I stepped to the side as he entered, his large frame filling the doorway. "Those are beautiful."

"Hmm." He bent and brushed a kiss across my lips, sending a ripple effect of sparks from where we touched. "I had inspiration."

Heat climbed my cheeks, and I grinned at his compliment. The flowers were stunning, a mix of wildflowers, lilies, and deep-red roses. "Are these from Cat's shop?"

He placed a bag on the counter, and mouthwatering smells from the food he'd picked up filled the kitchen. "They are. I dropped off a bouquet to her too."

My heart melted. "I bet she was beyond pleased."

He winked then pulled me in for a hug. "I missed you."

I rested my head on his chest and let the stress of the day evaporate. His scent surrounded me, and I breathed him in, wishing we could remain like that for the rest of the night. The passionate kisses were amazing, but I always wanted more. I wanted all of him, and tonight was no different. The growl from his stomach had me tilting my head back and grinning at him. "Hungry?"

"Starved." His dilated pupils insinuated a dual meaning, and butterflies took flight in my stomach.

The weather was unseasonably warm, and I didn't want to remain inside. We dished up lasagna and a chopped salad, setting everything on a tray with a bottle of Sangiovese. I carried the red wine glasses, and he brought everything else. Once we were seated around the grotto's small table, lapping waves and salty air added to the atmosphere I craved. The temptation to spend as much time out there was hard to resist.

We chatted about his day and my work on the mural, enjoying the peaceful grotto and good wine. Once the food was gone, his arm went around my shoulders, and I leaned into him as we finished our second glass of wine.

"I've never been so content in my entire life." His deep voice rumbled from his chest. "Even though we haven't known each other for that long, there's no doubt in my mind that you're the one for me."

We drew apart enough so that we were face to face, and he brushed the pad of his thumb over the curve of my lower lip. "I love you, Gianna. I can't imagine a day without you in it."

My eyes misted, and I cleared my throat, temporarily holding the too-close-to-the-surface emotions at bay so I could convey my similar thoughts. "From the time you saved me, our first meeting at the café, my feelings for you have only grown. I love you, too, Sergio."

His sinful lips curved into a smile. "I know it's early and we're basically already doing this, but this just feels right to officially ask you. Will you move to the third floor and stay with me here? As well as share my home in Rome?"

"Yes." I worried my lower lip with my teeth. *Does he mean until I'm finished with my job for Francesca?*

"I can see the wheels turning. What are you thinking?"

I shrugged. "Just that I'll be done with the project in a few days."

"For now, I'd be happy if you agreed to stay with me on the third floor. When your work on the fresco is done, I'd love for you to stay with me and not go back to the States." His serious gaze bore into mine, and the sincerity I read there stole my breath. "I want to fall asleep with you in my arms and wake with your gorgeous face as the first thing I see in the mornings. We can figure out the details of where you want to live, here or in Rome, later. Even traveling back and forth when I need to or staying here if you have work to do in Venice. Is this something you want too?"

"With all my heart."

He pulled me into his lap, his hands tangling in my hair as he cupped my head. Our lips came together in mutual need, a burst of love that exposed the primal connection we shared. The bold black currant and oaky flavors of the Sangiovese threaded through in a kiss that was the finest I'd ever tasted. I lost myself to the moment, to his expert ministrations. We momentarily broke apart, and the space around me faded so that all I could see was the handsome man before me.

"I can't stop thinking about you…" His features were taut with raw of emotion. "I can't fully explain it, but it's as if I'm drowning when you're not near. And I have this irrational fear that you'll leave me but not of your own will. That something is going to happen to you. It makes me crazy."

The murmur of voices sounded as the swoosh of a gondola sailed by the opening to the alcove. I shook my head, my gaze locked on his. "Nothing will. I'm here and not going anywhere." I'd made my decision. I wasn't returning to the

States. Venice or wherever Sergio was was where I was meant to be, where I was complete.

He pulled me closer. Pressed against him, I was incapable of uttering a word. His lips grazed over mine again, and my eyelids closed. From the first moment he'd held me when I'd fallen mysteriously ill at the end of my first gondola tour, I'd longed to feel his touch again.

Every moment we spent together, each touch and caress, would never be enough.

My head spun as he deepened the kiss, exploring, taking his time. The banked embers of desire stirred to life, raging through my body. I wanted—needed—him. Without breaking the kiss, he stood and swept me into his arms, and my legs automatically wrapped around his waist. Then we were moving, but I didn't care where, so long as he didn't stop kissing me.

We bumped into the corner of the couch, and he growled. The world around us trickled back in, and I broke our kiss. As I pulled back to laugh, I sucked in a breath instead, the amusement getting caught in my throat. Intense need pulled his features taut, and desire darkened his warm brown eyes, the expansion of his pupils all but eclipsing them. He pivoted from the couch and carried me to the kitchen. When he eased me onto the island, the cold press of the stone cooled my heated flesh through my skirt.

I threaded my fingers through his thick hair, my nails scraping against his scalp as I molded myself to him then slanted my mouth over his in a kiss that told him how heated I was. He bunched the fabric of my skirt up over my thighs to pool at my waist, trailing his fingers along my sensitive inner thighs. When he traced the edge of my panties, I struggled to breathe. Heat pooled low, and I moaned as the pad of his thumb grazed over the sensitive bundle of nerves at the apex of my thighs, the slip of silk frustratingly in our way.

When his lips left mine, I gasped, and my world spun. The clothes between us were offensive, and I wanted them gone. My fingers worked the buttons on his shirt until they were undone. The fabric splayed open, I took in his impressive chest. Absently, I pushed the shirt from his shoulders. Then his was kissing me again, and all thought fled. The touch of his hand at the side of my face melted my heart, as did the way his lips caressed mine, sending a volley of electric shocks throughout my body. I couldn't get enough of him. My arms wrapped around his neck, and my fingers curled in his hair, the soft strands just long enough to grip.

He brushed a thumb across my kiss-swollen bottom lip before tucking a long strand of hair behind my ear. I shivered as his fingers trailed down my cheek and rested on the pulse fluttering at the base. "You're everything to me, Gianna. I love you."

My breath caught in my throat, and I felt a lifetime of love for him swell within me. A fine sheen of tears coated my eyes at the intensity of the moment we shared. "I love you too. More than I could ever adequately express." I wanted a lifetime of moments with him, where every time was as powerful as our first.

The poignant moment took what was happening between us to another level. Passion smoldered in his dark eyes, and I lost myself in his touch. He lifted me enough to tug my skirt and panties down my legs. There was nothing between my bare skin and the chilly island's stone countertop. I reached for the waistband of his pants, but he stilled my hand.

"Not yet." His deep voice sent a volley of shivers across my exposed skin.

We were both half naked, me from the waist down and his chest bare. I sensed he was going to take things slowly, escalating his caresses. But that wasn't what I wanted, not this time. I let everything I wanted flame to life in my gaze.

He sucked in a breath, and we were kissing again, his mouth commanding mine in an explosion of desire. When he angled my head to deepen the kiss, I moaned. My fingers bit into his broad shoulders, tugging him impossibly closer. I couldn't get enough of him.

The sensation of my bare skin against the fabric of his pants was both frustrating and erotic, heightening my need to touch all of him. His hand skimmed down the curve of my back, and I shivered, arching against him, wanting to climb inside his skin. I couldn't get close enough.

When he pulled back, I felt the loss immediately, my gaze jerking to his. The kiss of chilly air to my exposed skin caused goose bumps to dance along my body. I needed his heat and the weight of him more than I needed air to breathe.

"You're so beautiful."

I shivered at the reverence in his tone. With unhurried movements, he lifted and resettled me so that I leaned back on my elbows, my legs spread wide and partially draping over his shoulders. I visually devoured every inch of him that I could as anticipation built. I didn't have to wait long. The first touch of his lips to my inner thigh kicked my pulse into a fast percussion. When he teased the sensitive flesh that yearned for his touch, a breathy moan slipped past my parted lips.

I wanted him almost desperately. Then he kissed me there, his fingers pushing inside, filling me, thrusting in and out as his mouth worked magic. Everything but what he was doing to me faded, my body flushed and oversensitive to his every ministration.

I watched his dark head between my legs. Sensations built, and heat exploded inside me. His fingers curled deep inside, and my head fell to the island. There was no holding back. Waves of ecstasy crashed over me as he increased the friction of his mouth against my highly sensitive bundle of nerves. My back arched, and stars exploded behind my eyes as he took me over the edge.

Boneless, I lay there, unable to move. Then Sergio swept me into his arms once again. As the world trickled back into focus, I became aware of the bedroom he'd carried me into. My legs slid down his body, but he held me to him.

"Can you stand?"

I barely recognized the hoarse passion filling voice. I nodded yes, and he released his hold only to ease my shirt and bra from my body. I wavered on my feet. Desire flamed back to life with a rush of heat to my core. Wanting to help, I tugged at his belt, but he gently brushed my fingers aside then lifted me onto the bed, the plush mattress cushioning my body.

He made quick work of the rest of his clothes then joined me on the bed, and I welcomed his weight.

I wanted him, now and always. My hand skimmed along his hip as I shifted my legs to fully cradle him between them. I traced the taut muscles of his shoulders and back as they dipped and flexed beneath my fingers. I reached the dip between his shoulder blades and applied pressure in an attempt to draw him closer.

I shivered from the dark promise in his eyes. He crowded me, heat radiating from him. With excruciating slowness, his hand moved up the outer side of my thigh. I quivered with barely banked desire as he trailed kisses along my neck. Anticipation built, and I whimpered, needing him to fill me. My fingers trailed higher, twisting in the strands of his hair at the nape of his neck. With a moan, I wound my leg around his waist, urging him closer as I squirmed against the hard length of him, desperate to increase the friction.

The scrape of his teeth where my neck met my shoulder had me arching against him, crying out as intoxicating sensations burst along every inch of skin that he caressed. The hard press of him against my body caused me to squirm with need. The deep growl that rumbled through his chest and against mine provoked a heady sense of power—I was able to affect him in the same manner that he did me. His hand cupped my hip, stilling me from pressing against him, taking control once again.

My neck arched, giving him greater access as his kisses trailed over the sensitive skin until his lips brushed back and forth over mine, and I melted against him.

With each caress, jolts of desire spread through my already heated body. I didn't know how much longer I could take it. I flattened my hands over his shoulders as he shifted, his hard length pressed against my thigh. Leashed strength rippled under my fingertips. Teasing and insistent, he deepened the kiss. My body hummed from his touch, and my core exploded with heat, slicking the way for his entry. Dizzy with want, I arched against him and moaned as he pushed against my entrance.

I couldn't wait much longer, my body hypersensitive as desire built to uncontrollable heights. His kisses and caresses escalated with our need for one another, and I dug my nails into his shoulders, urging him on.

"Sergio." His name was a plea, a benediction, when his lips left mine. Our gazes locked, and I read a frenzied passion that equaled mine in his dilated eyes. I shook with need, with anticipation. "I want you. Now."

"You drive me crazy, Gianna. I can never get enough of you." He pressed against my core as our lust-filled gazes locked together, and I arched against him. As he filled me, sensations exploded, and I cried out at the rightness of it, my body convulsing around him as he claimed my mouth in a searing kiss.

My fingers dug into his back as his corded muscles flexed

and bulged. We moved together, our breaths quickening as the sensations built between us with each powerful thrust. My nails bit into him as I neared another climax. Then his hand was between us, dipping between my folds. My head rocked back against the pillow as he teased the sensitive nerves until I cried out. My eyes squeezed shut as cresting waves of light burst behind my lids, and my body squeezed his, convulsing around him.

His movements quickened, heightening the explosive passion between us as he chased my climax with his own. As we drifted down from the frenzied heights of passion, he dipped his head to my neck, trailing kisses along the curve, and I moaned his name. When he whispered mine, the sound vibrated against my skin, and a shiver chased the decadence of it. I clung to him, shaken as I always was by the connection we shared.

When he pulled out, I felt the loss instantly. I didn't want him to move when he shifted to the side, rolling me with him. I didn't mind his weight over me and told him so.

He reached for the sheet then the duvet and pulled them over us. He tugged me back against him, and I snuggled closer, my body sated. I tangled my legs with his, my cheek resting on his chest, and he traced soothing circles along my back with an unhurried touch.

My eyelids closed, and I relaxed deeply within the protection of his embrace. Well loved and content, I drifted, tiptoeing into my dreams, sure in the knowledge that come morning, I would wake in his arms.

CHAPTER 16

*A*s darkness filled the corner of our bedroom where the moonlight didn't reach, Sergio's warmth seeped into me. My breathing synced with the steady rise and fall of his impressive chest and lured me into a peaceful sleep. In his arms, I found peace. Hours must have passed, and we shifted. The faint strains of violins teased my ear, and I turned onto my side, away from the heat Sergio's body provided. A chill stole under the covers and slithered over my skin, but the mesmerizing notes of a symphony held me immobile as obscure images invaded my mind and pulled me deeper into a dream or a memory.

As had happened the night before, my soul stretched its wings, and I was once again caught in Sophia's world and the evening when her fiancé, Edoardo, found her at the festival.

Tears filled my eyes at the tight grip Edoardo had on my upper arm. My skirts swirled around my legs and brushed against his trouser-clad one as he pulled me roughly through the crowd of artfully dressed partygoers. Distance grew between Giovanni and me. I felt the loss acutely.

In a desperate attempt to get help, I risked looking over my shoulder to see if my love was following, if he would rescue me. There were too many people, and it became darker the farther we traveled from the Piazza San Marco.

Something terrible was going to happen. I could feel it deep in my bones. He yanked hard on my arm, sending pain spiraling into my shoulder as we separated from the rest of the crowd to a café's canal-side patio. "Edoardo, please stop. You're hurting me!"

A low growl rumbled from his barrel chest as we broke through the vast horde of people. My gaze darted around, looking for an exit. What is he going to do? Fear like nothing I'd ever experienced before licked over my body like an icy flame.

My feet tangled, and I would have gone down if not for the way my fiancé dragged me with his punishing grip. There was no one around, and true terror infused every cell of my being. He could do anything to me, and no one would know. Find me, Giovanni. I chanted the urgent plea over and over in my mind.

Edoardo whirled me around to face him, clamping both of his meaty hands on my upper arms. Trapped, my gaze locked on his, he barked menacingly through sneering lips. "You betrayed me."

With each word, he shook my body, rattling my teeth with the force. "I—"

"Do not lie to me, Sophia. I saw you with him. Yesterday, at the beach."

Oh, God. I'd thought we were safe. I couldn't have been more wrong. My heart fractured at the sure knowledge of how I would never see Giovanni again if I even made it to tomorrow, as I was experiencing Edoardo's legendary temper.

Fury transformed Edoardo's face into a monstrous mask of hatred. His bellow echoed off the nearby water's surface and stole my breath. "If I can't have you, then no one can!" he roared as he shoved me hard. My body flew back toward the canal. Pain exploded, and my vision went dark.

With a gasp, I jerked into a sitting position. My hands clutched the bedsheets, grounding me into the fact that what

I'd just experienced was a dream or perhaps a deeply buried memory of the past—Sophia's, not mine.

Tremors wracked every inch of me before I was enveloped in strong arms and a familiar scent. Sergio.

"I've got you." His soothing deep baritone wrapped around me. "It was just a dream."

I wasn't so sure it was. The remnants of the horror of what happened chilled me to the point that I gripped Sergio's bicep, my nails digging in and forming crescent-shaped dents. Forcing myself to breathe, I rested my head on his chest. I let him coax me to lie down, still firmly within his embrace. His hand trailed along my back, easing the fear and worry away.

"Do you want to talk about it?"

Do I? I worried my lower lip, suppressing the terror squatting inside me. "Part of me does. The other half doesn't want to relive it." I wanted to tell him what I suspected, that it was Sophia's memories, but I didn't want to dive back in to what I'd seen in such vivid detail again. "Maybe later?" Not only that, but I finally understood my intense reaction my second day in Venice when my gondolier, Antonio, had pulled onside Osteria Al Squero's dock and I doubled over from acute head pain. It was where Sophia's head had struck a gondola before she sank into the watery arms of the canal.

He accepted my decision not to talk about it, and we lay there for several more seconds as the dream faded and the room slowly lightened, a clear sign of the new day. A sense of peace washed over me as the nightmare faded further. Neither of us had gone back to sleep, and after a few more minutes, Sergio broke the comfortable silence between us.

"I'm going to get the coffee started and make some eggs. Are you hungry?"

I brushed a thick lock of dark hair from his forehead, smiling at the sexy image of him first thing in the morning. If not for the nightmare, it would have been another perfectly shared moment. "Yes, and I would love some breakfast. I'll be there in a minute." I wanted to brush my teeth and take a quick shower.

After my shower, I towel dried my hair and got dressed. Then I let the heavenly smell of coffee guide me to the small kitchenette on the opposite side of the spacious floor. Curious, I glanced around the inviting room. It was done in the same cream-and-tan tones and felt timeless. Beautiful Italian décor and intricate crown molding blended in seamless harmony. The kitchen was small and new, clearly installed relatively recently to accommodate apartment-style living on the floor.

I came up behind Sergio and wrapped my arms around his narrow waist, resting my head against his broad back. My eyelids fluttered, and when he covered my hands with his, I smiled at the sheer love and contentment that radiated between us. It was where I was meant to be.

All my life, I'd felt the pull to Venice, and I couldn't help but think again that fate had a hand in taking me there, and that we were destined to find one another.

We parted, and I helped him carry the food and much-needed coffee to the round table off the kitchenette. He'd made a fluffy omelet, which filled me up, and I sipped my drink, contemplating my plan for the day. I had to work on the mural but agreed to take part of the day off to spend with him. Soon, he would be going back to Rome for appointments, and I would remain behind. I would have loads of time to finish the mural, especially for the few inches of repair needed at the bottom. I thought through the process of applying a solution to dampen the plaster so it was malleable enough to apply the tints in a watercolor manner. Once it dried, the paint would adhere to the plaster.

Sergio leaned back in his chair. "I thought we could check

in with Adriano this morning and see if your dress is ready for the masquerade dinner."

"That sounds great. When are we going to the party? It's a weekend event, isn't it?"

"It is. I'm hoping only to be gone a day or two, due to patient appointments. I'll be back for sure on Saturday, the night of the event."

"That'll give me time to get more work done on the mural." I would maximize my time to get ahead while he was away. "The island has gotten busier." With the influx of tourists, there was foot traffic everywhere, making it a challenge to move through the streets. I preferred Venice when there wasn't an event like the one coming up and the tourism was more manageable.

We cleaned the dishes, and while he showered, I returned to the first floor for clean clothes. I planned to bring a few things up to his closet, but I was a little unsure what we would do in terms of living arrangements, something we would have to talk about in more detail one night over a glass or two of wine. Even though he'd asked me to move in with him and I'd accepted, I couldn't accompany him every time he had to go to Rome.

Part of me wanted to remain in Venice, but I also enjoyed Rome. Maybe when I finished the mural, we could do what he was already doing and travel back and forth, so long as I could figure out how to manage working.

For the first time since we shared the same residence, Sergio used the interior stairwell when I was on the first floor, and I quite liked it. I turned from gazing out the windows at the canal to smile at him. My heart skipped a beat, and those familiar butterflies took flight in my stomach at the sight of him. His larger-than-life presence filled the space.

"Ready?" His dark-brown eyes sparkled, and he tugged me to him for a breathtaking kiss.

When we broke apart, I nodded as the world inched back into focus. Hand in hand, we exited the residence. I glanced back to see if Cat was on her dock. "Cat isn't outside this morning. I hope she's okay."

"We're running a little late. She was probably already outside, and we just missed her."

I hadn't even checked the clock. When I was around Sergio, I always lost track of time. The older woman had become a good friend, though, and I worried about her. I was just glad that the Dellucci family made a point to spend time with her as well.

We wandered the streets, talking about what I wanted to do with my career and if I wanted to focus on restorations or continue with my own artwork. There was no pressure from Sergio, and I found myself able to think of my painting in terms of fulfillment rather than what would bring in the most income.

He'd made it clear that the expenses were covered wherever we lived, and I wouldn't have to worry about that. It was freeing, and while I would typically have rejected relying on someone else, it wasn't like that with him. Loving him was so ingrained in every aspect of my being that sharing what we had between us for the best life was natural. There was no power play, no resentment, no expectations other than to make one another happy.

Sergio pointed out several places he and his brother used to go when they were younger as we meandered through the streets.

"Tell me some of Venice's ghost stories." The weight of centuries was in every building and district we walked by.

We were momentarily distracted as we rounded a corner and came across a bride and groom across the canal. Her groom held her fast in his arms as her simple satin gown draped over the small ledge they stood on, trailing into a moored gondola rather than the water that surrounded it. Their poignant moment was captured by a photographer on our side of the canal, while another snapped photographs from his perch on a nearby bridge. I couldn't help but be caught up in the magic of the moment. "I wonder how many brides and grooms have stood in that very spot."

A breeze ruffled Sergio's dark hair, and he gave my fingers a light squeeze. "Have you heard of Tosca?"

"No, I haven't." We continued to stroll through the maze of streets with Sergio navigating the way to Adriano Atelier, Adriano and David's clothing store.

"Hers is a story of love and death." He played with a sterling silver ring I wore on my pinky finger, twisting it this way and that. "Tosca lived in the fourteenth century, and while very beautiful, she was poor. It seemed her luck changed when she became engaged to a wealthy nobleman whom she did not love."

"Did she go through with the wedding, then?" I couldn't imagine marrying for any reason other than love.

He pulled me closer as we sidestepped a family who were eyeing a bakery rather than paying attention to where they were going. "No. When she met someone else and fell in love with him, they stole away to Venice. But they didn't find the sanctuary they sought because her fiancé located them. In a fit of jealousy, he murdered Tosca's lover and cut off her ring finger, swearing that no one could have her if he couldn't."

I shivered at the idea of what the young woman had experienced.

"Not long after, she took her life. Since that time, there have been sightings of the young bride searching for her ring finger as she roams through Venice's maze of streets."

I tilted my head back to meet Sergio's gaze. "Have you ever seen her?"

"No." He bent and pressed a too short kiss to my lips. "And for that, I'm grateful."

We turned onto the winding street where Adriano's shop was, and I pushed the sad story from my mind as excitement sizzled in anticipation of what Adriano had made for me to wear to the festival. As soon as we stepped through the door to the tinkle of the overhead bell, David turned toward us with an ear-to-ear grin. After answering another customer's question, he hurried over, enveloped us both in hugs, then tugged us past rows of exquisite gowns in every hue and toward the dressing area.

I felt as if I had whiplash, trying to take it all in until Adriano spotted us. More hugs were given, and he rushed me to a changing room, where he'd hung the gown in a garment bag on a hook. With infinite slowness, I slid the zipper down then parted the bag. One blink, then two, and I stumbled back. After slamming into the wall of the changing room, I slid down to my butt. My heart pounded, and saliva pooled in my mouth. Frantically swallowing continuous streams so I didn't vomit in Adriano's shop, I worked to inhale slowly through my nose to the volley of frantic knocks on the door.

"What happened? Are you all right?"

I needed to get myself together. "Yes, totally fine. Just lost my balance trying to get the dress on. Nothing's ripped. Just give me a second."

"Gianna." Sergio's concern clung to his deep voice.

I got control of myself, and the saliva stopped pooling in my mouth. I responded with more confidence than I felt. "I'm okay, really."

I took my time removing the show-stopping gown from the bag. Deep-red satin, lace, and tiny black beads formed a dress that would normally have been almost any woman's dream. To me, it held a mixture of hope and devastation because the dress that Adriano swore was made for me was the one I'd seen in my vision the last time Sergio and I had been there. It wasn't made for me but for Sophia. It was her dress, and I was going to wear it to a party that mimicked the festival she'd attended while hoping to run away with Giovanni.

Sergio waited on the strategically positioned couch that faced a raised platform in front of a half-circle of mirrors for my reentrance. I smoothed my hand down the crimson satin behind the closed door to the dressing room. Despite the fact that Sophia's dress was the same or at least very similar, I enjoyed the moment for what it was. I didn't think I'd ever seen something so beautiful, nor had I owned a dress like that. As I changed into the gown, the image of myself in the room's floor-length mirror blurred the edges of time. It was as if it had been made for me, and in the recesses of my mind, I knew it was always meant to be mine.

CHAPTER 17

I sat across Cat's canal-side table on her enticing dock in the early morning, taking one of the only relaxing moments I would enjoy that day. I planned to finish the third panel, no matter how late I had to work. I inhaled the fragrant air and soaked up the peacefulness of having coffee with Cat. As I was situated right next door, visiting with her so often was easy. The abundance of greenery in November made the experience that much more special.

I wouldn't have minded making the Marcello home a permanent residence. So far, I loved living with Sergio. Waking in his arms was the perfect way to start my day. We'd gotten up early together, and I wished he hadn't had to leave for an emergency appointment that was moved up, but he would be back the next day.

"Try one." Cat urged as she pushed a plate of tempting croissants closer. "These are Francesca's favorite."

After accepting one and taking a bite, I smiled my agreement about how good it was. Flaky and buttery, it was indeed a wonderful way to begin the day. "Mine too."

"Lorenzo and I would have a croissant and coffee every

morning before he went to work in the flower shop. Most Venetians go to the Grancaffè Quadri in Piazza San Marco every morning, but I loved to bake and would make these croissants for us and steal a few more minutes together."

"That's a lovely tradition, Cat."

"Hmm." She took a sip of her coffee. "Something to think about, Bella. Life passes us by in a handful of moments. Gather as many as you can with Sergio and make a lifetime of treasured memories."

I squeezed her hand then noticed Lucia and Daniela emerging from their home and heading our way. Everything in me froze. That woman rubbed me the wrong way, and I would have preferred to avoid her. Daniela offered up a breezy wave. *Please don't join us.* I pasted on a smile that I hoped didn't come across as forced.

Lucia's expression pinched as her dark gaze landed on me, her smile insincere. Daniela floated over in her cheery way, plopping down after giving Cat a one-armed hug. She turned to me with a sparkle in her expressive light-brown eyes. "Adriano is working nonstop with last-minute requests for the festival, but he snapped me a pic of your gown." She clicked the picture icon on her phone. "I have a screenshot." She tapped on the image then showed it to both Cat and Lucia.

Cat sucked in a breath. Her gaze darted from me to the picture, and the color leached from her parchment cheeks. Lucia's lips thinned, and she shared a pained look with Cat. When she fully turned to me, barely disguised anger was tenaciously leashed at best. "You should be careful," Lucia warned. "History has a way of repeating itself."

I didn't have a comeback, as I was very aware of what they were talking about. The dress was the same one that Sophia had worn, and things had not turned out well for her.

Daniela saved me from answering with an annoyed look

at her mom before taking over the conversation. "It's beautiful, and I can't wait to see you in it."

"Are you going as well?" It would be nice to see a few other people I knew there. For some reason, I felt a mixture of both excitement and dread over the event.

"I am." Daniela grinned. "Adriano made a royal-blue one for me with a matching mask. I'm going with a group of friends. I'm assuming Sergio is taking you?"

"Yes." My shoulders relaxed the more we chatted. It was clear there was no animosity between us over my dating Sergio. Lucia, on the other hand… I stole a glance at her furious expression.

"I'll find you." Daniela squeezed me in a hug.

"We need to get going, Daniela." Lucia said a hasty goodbye before giving us her back.

Daniela's smile was apologetic as she hurried to catch up to her mother. Seconds passed while Cat and I eyed their retreating forms.

"There are a lot of things Lucia struggles with." Cat patted my hand before slipping another croissant onto my plate. They were so good that I couldn't resist. "Try not to take her seriously."

"It's hard not to." The very fact that Cat had said that to me before should have told me that the fault lay at Lucia's feet. But whatever, I would try to do as she asked. I brushed a few flaky crumbs from my shirt.

Cat sighed, her gaze turning speculative as the gentle breeze lifted a few strands of her long silver hair and swept it back. "I believe she views you as the other woman, something she's had firsthand experience with because of Antoinette. And in her mind, she'd already married Daniela to Sergio, even though they only went on a handful of dates."

"Was there a chance of Sergio and Daniela becoming

more?" My stomach soured at the thought, and I set my half-eaten croissant back on the plate, no longer hungry.

"No. It was all in Lucia's head. If history repeats itself, it's because of her willing it so. You have nothing to worry over, Bella."

Perhaps. But my gut hadn't settled, and whatever the reason for Lucia's deep-seated animosity toward me, I wasn't going to take it lightly.

CHAPTER 18

With my phone pressed to my ear, I stepped back to survey the exterior wall of the Marcello residence, where I was getting ready to work on the fresco. It was a pretty monumental moment, and I wanted to share it with the woman who had hired me to complete it. Francesca answered on the third ring.

"Gianna, what a pleasant surprise."

"I wanted to call and share that I'm working on the third panel today. It'll be finished by tomorrow." I couldn't have kept the smile from my voice if I tried.

"Oh my." Francesca squealed. "I wish I was there to see it, but I'll be home soon. Hopefully in two days, if I can get my travel sorted."

We chatted for a few more moments before saying goodbye for the time being. I couldn't wait to get to work. As I finished getting set up, the familiar thrill of excitement over a nearly completed project hummed through my veins.

The smell of paint and plaster saturated the air before being whisked away on a breeze off the canal. Even though I missed Sergio, I'd enjoyed my breakfast and coffee with Cat before Lucia's veiled warning. The morning passed in a blur. I hadn't minded that Sergio had to return to Rome for that appointment, as it enabled me to work on the mural.

I'd planned to go until the light faded and had even set up spotlights I'd rented from the paint store to allow me to continue. I took a moment to take in the painting and the progress I'd made so far.

I'd sketched the design, tweaked it, then traced it with the end of a fine-tipped paintbrush onto where damp Venetian plaster waited. With the tints already mixed with water, I'd set to work painting over the plaster, needing to have the scene completed in a matter of twelve or so short hours, since the weather was cooperating. It wasn't too cold but cool enough to prolong the curing process. Once the chemical change occurred, the pigments would bind to the plaster.

The Trevi Fountain, what Sergio envisioned as the final panel, had taken shape and glistened in the glow of the scene's moonlight. It looked so similar to what we'd done together.

There was more than one legend attached to the fountain, but like Sergio, I preferred the one about the lovers. Not for the first time, I felt as though I was walking in footsteps that I'd already traveled. A fragrant breeze swept along, and I brushed back the strands of hair that danced in the wind and tickled my face. As the sun beat overhead, my stomach growled, and I headed in to eat a quick sandwich.

I made a panini, put it on a plate, and walked up to the fourth level to look again at Il Verrocchio's paintings. Sergio had shown me several hanging upstairs, but I wanted another view.

Where the ceiling met the wall was an unobtrusive and slim mounting rail. Wires hung from the support system with a clip screw that secured the framed pictures and paintings.

Sitting on the couch, I gazed at the incredible impression-istic seascape and canal renditions that showcased why people fell in love with Venice. Romance fairly bled from the artwork. Working with his mural and viewing his pieces was like knowing an intimate part of the man he'd been. I wished I could have met him in person. Part of me knew I had.

Francesca had been right. My work bore a striking resemblance to Il Verrocchio's. I felt more connected to him than I had on any other artist's restoration projects.

I finished the last bite of my food and washed it down with Pellegrino. It was time to get back to work, as I only had a narrow window to complete the third panel before the Venetian plaster cured. I stood to do just that when I noticed a small painting unlike the others. It was of a café with canal-side tables, done in dark colors and brushstrokes that trans-mitted pain and despair. It was empty, devoid of life.

I peered closer. *That looks familiar.* I recognized the patio, the glimpse of boutiques across the way, and the width of the canal. *This can't be a coincidence.* I pulled my phone from my pocket and thumbed through the pictures I'd taken since arriving in Venice.

My pulse pounded loudly in my ears. It wasn't until the beginning of the series that I saw it. I hadn't been sure if I'd caught the café during the gondola ride. I had. The image after the panoramic view took my breath away. It must have been taken by accident when the gondolier handed my phone and purse to Sergio while he'd held me.

Even off-center, we were within the camera frame, if not slightly blurry. *Oh God.* Sergio's arms were wrapped around me while my head rested against his solid chest.

That wasn't what had me riveted in place. It was the glowing sunspots that hovered near our heads.

CHAPTER 19

I'd spent a restless night tossing and turning. The wait for daylight and Sergio's return had made sleep impossible. The sense of satisfaction that should have carried throughout the night and into the day dimmed against my preoccupation over speaking with him. Nevertheless, I spent the time alone, photographing the fresco's completion and tidying the inside of the house while revisiting what had happened upon my arrival in Venice.

The weird symptoms occurred the first time I arrived at the café, and the uncanny recognition of everything had made more sense as Sophia showed me snippets of her life and experiences through dreams or visions. I checked the time. *Sergio will be here soon.* I tapped my fingernail against my phone, restless and impatient for when I would leave to meet him for dinner at the café.

Since I'd set foot on the floating city, I'd had a sense of homecoming, and I had become convinced, more than ever, that I'd lived there before. It was perhaps in another life but one spent in Venice.

The couple depicted on the mural I'd restored haunted

me. At first, their faces had been a mystery, their profiles the only hint of who they were. Her dark hair was swept into an updo, accentuating the curve of her neck. I was fascinated with the way his hand was frozen for all time as he caressed her cheek. I knew it was Giovanni, but I wanted the physical proof. I had to know. It was the final puzzle piece that I would no longer be able to deny—the dreams and visions were memories. They were real and quite possibly my own from another lifetime.

I raced upstairs to the fourth floor, the one where Il Verrocchio had lived during his lifetime. I needed to see a picture of him, to be among things he'd touched. Sergio had said that not much had changed since then, aside from the replacement of heavy drapes and the upholstery, which had rotted in the sun over time.

Once I cleared the door, my feet moved seemingly of their own accord. I parted the drapes, and afternoon sunlight flooded the room. A panoramic view of the home across the way and the Grand Canal could be seen from the large trio of windows. An easel stood off to the side. Two couches were positioned before the windows, and between them sat a small ornate table.

I dropped to the couch next to the table, where several small silver frames rested. I hadn't looked at them the time Sergio brought me up here. The pictures behind the glass had turned from black and white to sepia. They were still in good condition, so the glass had to have been acid-free and sun resistant, given how well they'd protected the old photos. I figured the frames had been changed sometime recently.

The one closest to me was of a family. I guessed the adults to be Sergio's great-great-grandparents. I didn't know much about Sergio and Francesca's ancestors, other than the fact that he had an older brother. I replaced the family photo then picked one up that depicted two boys who were maybe in their twenties. My hand shook. *He looks so familiar.* It shouldn't have been a shock. I swapped the one of the two boys with a portrait of one of them. He wasn't a boy. He was a man. My breath caught and held. *It's him.*

I took the portrait closer to the window then noticed a smaller frame. *It can't be.* I rushed over to compare the portrait to one of a couple. *Same man, just a tad older.* The miniature photo was of a man smiling as he gazed down at a woman. My heart stilled. *I know his profile.* I'd yet to see her other than the time in the mirror, but I wanted physical proof. My greedy gaze skimmed the rest of the pictures until I found one that was taken of him closer to the age he had been when he died.

He had the same aristocratic nose, dark hair that defied the style he wore, and a mischievous smile that surely captured hearts in its wake. The picture was black and white, but I was sure his eyes were gray.

I'd met him my first night in Venice, lost in the fog. I had the confirmation I'd hoped to find. Everything that had been revealed to me through their spirits was true.

Giovanni.

Tremors racked my body, and I dropped onto the couch, clutching both the picture of him and the one that showed her face—*Sophia*. She wore her dark hair in an intricate style. A few long wavy curls had escaped and hung to frame her classically beautiful face. I took in her features, and all the air whooshed from my lungs. Her profile was so familiar—it was my own.

What was startling to me wasn't how much Sergio and I resembled them, but that we could actually have been them.

CHAPTER 20

A gentle midday breeze stirred the loose tendrils of my hair that'd escaped my messy bun, and I pushed the dark-brown strands from my face. *Hurry up, Sergio.* I was impatient. I took a sip from the glass of wine the waitress had brought me, my second.

I must be crazy to entertain this. My first night in Venice, I'd met Giovanni's ghost… *his ghost.* I was still trying to wrap my head around that even though almost two months had passed since it happened.

He'd thought I was Sophia. *Am I? Was I?* The more I contemplated the idea, the more it made sense, but I didn't understand how it was possible.

I toyed with and disregarded different explanations, always arriving at the same one. All my life, I'd felt a deep connection to old paintings, particularly those from the Renaissance. Impressionism and Romanticism had captivated me at the onset of my career and had continued to do so. *Is there a deeper meaning? A reason why I feel tethered? Could it be because of Giovanni and his artistry?*

I restlessly tapped my fingers against the canal-side table-top. Sergio was due to arrive any minute, but I found it difficult to remain seated. I rose on feet that weren't quite steady and moved to the edge of the patio, where gondolas deposited passengers. There was a lull in activity except for a single boat.

A happy couple laughed, pointed out the café, then waved to a couple at a nearby table. A faint smile curved my lips. They must have been meeting friends. The distraction—any, really—helped. Without it, I would have continued to dive deeper into my absurd theory, which I was convinced couldn't possibly be correct.

I'd called Sergio while he was already heading to Venice from a meeting in Rome. I'd arrived early, needing to stretch my legs and think. The wine helped, too, lending a pleasant haze to my spiraling thoughts. My fingers splayed over the railing near the opening to the dock for gondola access that separated Osteria Al Squero's patio from the canal.

A loud crash of breaking glass clattered behind me, and I spun around. I turned too soon, and a waiter's tray collided with my head.

Pain exploded across my forehead. Alarmed voices faded in and out, and I stumbled backward from dizziness. My body went limp as the world blinked in and out. The wedge of my shoe landed on broken glass and slid out from under me, and I fell back, my hip hitting the corner of the rail where it ended and the opening for waterway boarding began. I was falling, and there was nothing I could do to stop my descent into the waiting water.

In a recess of my mind, I remembered that Sophia had died in the canal, and that there was there was a deep trench in that part of the waterway.

Strong arms wrapped around me, and I reached blindly for the arms that held me. Terror danced along my skin as I tried to lift a hand to my head. Pain throbbed across my forehead, and my vision went black.

SERGIO's familiar scent was the first thing that registered, calming me as I eased back into consciousness. Cradling me in his embrace, he shared the heat from his body, something I sorely needed. I'd kept my eyes closed, but I must have made a sound, alerting him that I was awake.

"You're safe." Sergio helped me sit up. Even with a blanket draped around me, I couldn't stop trembling.

He said something to the people who crowded around. I didn't know how long we sat like that. Clutched tightly against his chest, I tried to reassure myself that the outcome could have been worse. But the love of my life held me, protecting me from what could have happened. Eventually, the people backed up.

My fingers dug into his shoulders. I took deep breaths and calmed enough to pull back. His eyes held stark terror. *I could have drowned like she did.* I had to tell him. "Serg—"

"Shh… I've got you. A water taxi is on the way. We'll go to the hospital, and they can check you out there."

"No." I didn't want to go anywhere near the water, at least not right away, and definitely not to a hospital. My mind reeled from the experience I'd just had, which was so similar to *hers*. "My head hurts."

"It's just a bump." He sucked in a ragged breath, and his forehead rested against the side of my head while his hands cradled me to him. "I've never been so scared in my life."

There was irony there, and I tried to use it to lighten the mood. "You're a surgeon…" A violent tremor shook me again.

"None of my patients were you. It's different. Trust me."

I understood. Losing the love of one's life only invited darkness and despair. "I don't want to go to a hospital. Take me home. You can check me out to make sure I'm okay." I felt the tension in his body—he wanted to be sure. "I'm okay, Serg. Please. I want to go home."

When I felt better, we took a gondola home, arranged at no cost by the café—it was the least they could do, they said. Secure in Sergio's arms, I felt safe.

CHAPTER 21

Fresh from a shower and wrapped in both a blanket and Sergio's embrace, I reclined on the Marcellos' couch. He'd conducted a thorough exam and, with heavy cajoling from me, agreed to forego the hospital visit. I didn't have a concussion but did have a headache and a bump on my head. It could have been much worse. I was grateful he'd arrived when he had.

Sergio ran his fingers in soothing strokes through the strands of my towel-dried hair. "That was the most terrifying thing I've ever experienced, Gianna. I've never felt like that before. It was… world-ending."

Despair I understood. There was something about Venice that evoked emotion where I had no explanation—like the familiar experience of falling into the water. So many things reeked of fate.

He toyed with a strand of my hair, twisting it back and forth. "I have a confession to make."

I tilted my head to the side so I could see his face. "You do?"

"I was supposed to already have left for Rome that first day we met. I was stalling. I'd even pushed back my appointments, rescheduling them for the following day. There was no reason for it except this expectant sense that I couldn't leave, not yet."

I smiled. "There is something to that café. When I first arrived there and stepped off the gondola, the sickness that came over me crashed like a wave of fear and a splitting headache with no explanation. Then, in your arms, it left. I was perfectly fine. Other than being a little dizzy, a sense of peace and rightness came over me. So I do understand what you mean about our meeting. Oh!" I lurched up, and his arms fell away from my waist. "I asked you to meet me at the café today for a reason."

"What was it?"

"Your Aunt Francesca said something that seemed odd regarding the murals. I didn't question her at the time, but I think I'm beginning to understand." My fingers curled around the leather of my purse strap, and I dragged it into my lap. With a tug on the zipper, I slipped my hand inside and retrieved my phone.

"She can be that way. She has bouts of visions, premonitions that we have learned to trust." He sat up and angled his body so we were facing each other. "What did she say?"

"In response to my question about repairing the alcove mural, she said, 'The time isn't right. Soon, things will align, and they'll be home.' When I called her with questions about completing the final panel on the fresco mural, she told me to speak with you."

He shrugged. "I don't know how to explain it, but I've always known what Il Verrocchio would've painted."

"After we went to the Trevi Fountain and reenacted the legend of the lovers, it made perfect sense." *Please don't think*

I'm crazy. I tapped my fingernails against my phone's screen. "I went up to the fourth floor and looked at the family pictures. You never told me Il Verrocchio's real name was Giovanni or that his lover was Sophia." That wasn't entirely correct. "Well, you did, in a way, but not that I looked like Sophia."

"I…" His brows furrowed. "You're right. I never did. Aunt Francesca said something about not saying his name. I had no idea why, but I've learned to do as she says. You heard his name from Aunt Francesca?"

"You look so much like him." I ran my finger down the length of his slightly crooked nose. "Except here."

A small smile curved his lips. "It's odd. You resemble Sophia as well. I haven't thought about that for so long, not since I was young and not until you pointed out my resemblance to Giovanni."

I threaded my fingers with his. "I met him my first night in Venice. The fog was thick, and I got turned around. I heard a man calling for Sophia. His voice was heartbreaking, and I followed the sound and ended up at the same café where we met." I pressed the button to turn my screen on then handed it to him. "Look. I think the gondolier took this of us by accident when he handed you my phone."

His brows furrowed. "The sunspots."

"Yes." There were two of them. "I know this seems far-fetched, but so many things are familiar. How we felt for one another after we first touched… I think… could the light hovering near us be them?"

"It could mean that either of them was near."

I wanted to ask if we *were* them, but I thought better of it.

THE FOLLOWING NIGHT, Sergio took me to the nonprofit silent auction to preserve and restore Venice's reenactment dinner of the *Carnevale di Venezia*, the masquerade festival. It was by invitation only and something we were looking forward to, although I felt some trepidation about both Lucia's warning and wearing the dress.

As I stood before a floor-length mirror, wearing the deep-red and black lace-trimmed gown, a sense of euphoria swept over me, and the reflection blurred. I blinked several times, pushing away the feeling that I'd done the same thing before with a very similar dress, the festival, and the man. Hardening my resolve, I arranged my long hair so that it fell in waves along my back and gathered the sides to fasten near my nape with an antique silver clip.

Sergio emerged from the walk-in closet, dressed in a matching black gothic Victorian-style coat with cuffed sleeves and decorative buttons. The ruffled shirt matched the deep red of my dress, paired with black trousers. When his gaze met mine, his hands stilled, and I swear fire simmered in his dark eyes. My pulse went into overdrive, and that odd dizziness threatened, but I held onto the sight of him—he grounded me in the present, something I was so very grateful for. I wanted to be there with him, to experience everything to its fullest.

"You're stunning, Gianna." In two strides, he was in front of me, my hands in his as his gaze locked on mine, his pupils eclipsing the warm brown of his eyes. "I have a strong urge to keep you here all to myself. We could dine in our alcove." One hand settled on my hip, and the other cupped the side of my neck, his thumb caressing the curve of my jaw. "After, I would show you how you're the oxygen I need to breathe."

Heat infused my cheeks, and my hands convulsed around his waist. When I swayed as a wave of longing swept over me, he steadied me with the hand on my hip. The very idea of spending the evening just the two of us was almost impossible to resist, but… "I want that more than anything. Sadly, we can't. The fundraiser is important, and Adriano and David will be there. Daniela too."

The event was hosted by the very foundation that Francesca was involved with and that I entertained dreams of collaborating with one day. The theme was to come together in support of restoring, protecting, and preserving Venice. People all over Italy and known supporters of Venice, scattered across the globe, would be in attendance and taking part in the impromptu masquerade party and silent auction.

A war of emotions played across his features, furrowing his brows. I sensed the moment he made up his mind, and he tugged me closer. "I don't want to share you with anyone. There's something about tonight that makes me want to keep you close and never let you go."

My heart raced. My body relaxed against him, relieved that he felt it too. "Then don't. Let's make an appearance then leave as soon as we're able."

When he cupped my cheek and his thumb rubbed in a gentle caress back and forth, my eyelids fluttered closed, and I knew that leaving would be harder than I'd thought. A sense of impending doom lurked outside the door to the manor, a precursor we were both uncomfortably aware of. Deep in my bones, I knew that any association with the masquerade, the dress, and the two of us had dire consequences somewhere in our history, which was strange enough to think about, let alone lend a voice to.

Sergio groaned then put a few inches of distance between us. "Let me help you with your mask."

It was time. With trembling hands, I handed over the intricately designed scarlet mask, complete with hand-sewn black and silver beads. Adriano had deviated slightly from the hundred-year-old design to embellish bits of the present with three strands of light beads hanging in an evocative semicircle from ear to nose below the smaller cut of the demi-mask beneath my left eye.

When his all-black velvet mask accented with the same silver beads was secured, we left our bedroom and headed into the kitchenette the third floor offered. Two crystal goblets were on the counter, along with red wine. The wineglasses had been delivered as a thank-you gift from the foundation's board for our ticket purchase and attendance. The lovely bottle of Sangiovese was one Sergio and I had picked out when we'd stopped at Millevini on one of our evenings walks over the Rialto Bridge. A dainty silver wine charm hung around the stem with a number engraved on it in the shape of a mask that corresponded to our seats at one of the many tables. The color of the *contiere,* or Murano glass bead, which decorated the circular wire around the charm, also directed us to the appropriate table. Ours was gold, and the number on the mask charm was nineteen.

I slipped my black elbow-length satin gloves on while he busied himself by opening the wine. A soft suction sounded as Sergio withdrew the cork then filled our glasses. He handed one to me, and I fingered the dainty charm.

"Why do we both have the same number?"

"It was a way to honor the masquerade tradition as well as ensure the ticket holders' purchased place at the designated table is held. There will be two settings with the matching number of nineteen. Only the board members will know who the owners of the numbers are."

"That was smart." There had been a great deal behind anonymity in times past. Not knowing who people were hid social status and evened the playing field. It also opened doors to infidelity.

With both our masks in place and wine goblets in hand, we stepped into the crisp Venetian evening air.

"The mural. You captured the ambiance of the Trevi fountain perfectly." His voice whispered over my skin, and a shiver followed in its wake. "It's stunning. I meant to tell you when I saw it the other day but wanted to do so when we were together and in front of it."

Warmth filled me at the pride and reverence clear in his voice. "Thank you. I can't believe it's finished. It actually feels different out here."

He tilted his head, taking in the details of the third panel, and a smile flitted across his lips. "It's lighter. I can't put my finger on it, but it just feels right."

I agreed. It was as if something monumental had happened, and I wanted to think the finished panel freed Giovanni's troubled soul so that he could find Sophia after all those years.

Sergio locked the door, then we turned to make our way to the Piazza San Marco, where the fundraiser would be held. But Cat's warbled voice stopped us. As one, we turned and walked the handful of steps to her dock, where she, too, was enjoying a glass of wine.

"Don't you two look lovely tonight?" With a slowness that brought alarm, Cat pushed on the arms of the chair and stood. Once steady on her feet, she clasped her hands in mine. "It's uncanny."

I smiled, giving her hands a gentle squeeze. "What is?"

She released one of my hands and waved away the question. "Seeing you two brings back memories of past masquerade festivals is all."

"My apologies, Caterina." Sergio bowed over her hand, brushing a kiss over the back of her wrinkled hand. "I should have thought to invite you. If you would like to go, I can make a call to see if there are extra seats."

A pretty pink blush colored her cheeks, and her smile widened, adding a sparkle to her eyes that'd been missing. "That's very sweet, but I think I'll sit this one out. You two go and have a wonderful time."

Sergio and I took turns hugging her before saying our goodbyes then resumed our walk to the street that ran adjacent to our two properties. I tucked my arm in his and enjoyed seeing the other similarly dressed partygoers blending in with those out for an evening stroll but not going to the silent auction. There was a good mix of people attending, which was great for the foundation. A shiver skirted along my spine, causing a tremor to slosh the wine in my glass, and I pressed closer to Sergio.

He leaned close, and I shivered for a different reason. "Are you cold?"

When he shifted his wine to the hand where I clung to his arm and started to slip out of his jacket, I stopped him. "Just a little chill. I'm fine, though." I smiled up at him. "It was more of an anticipation shiver, I think."

Settling his ornate black coat back in place, he winked. "Other than dancing with you tonight, I'm looking forward to the evening being over so we can be alone."

My hand tightened on his bicep, the thought of what would transpire when we got back to the Marcello home sending a wave of heat through me, chasing the residual chill away. "I am too."

As we walked to Piazza San Marco, Sergio regaled me with tales of the trouble he and his brother got into when they were growing up. One story, in particular, was about Palazzo Contarini dal Zaffo in the *sestier* of Cannaregio, its origin dating back to the sixteenth century. The palace's annex was referred to as the House of Spirits.

"That building, like so many in Venice, is believed to be

haunted. Countless murders took place there, even one where a woman was chopped up, a portion of her body found by local fishermen. The palace and annex were cursed. One day, my brother and I wanted to tempt fate and were hanging out with our fishing poles dangling off the edge of the palace. Whenever anyone would stop to inform us of the grievous error of our ways and warn us of the dangers of the House of Spirits, we would nod and reply that we were aware and hoping to catch body parts, not fish."

"You didn't!" Horrified laughter over their antics spilled from my lips. "What did your parents do?"

"Luckily, Aunt Francesca intervened. She told the townspeople that we were ill and were supposed to be resting in bed. She said the dreadful tale was one we'd recently heard, and it must have infected our feverish minds, so pay no attention because she'd have us back in bed and nursed to health."

"Ah, she's full of mischief herself. And your parents?"

"Not as understanding. Aunt Francesca got a good laugh over it, but our parents grounded us for two weeks, and we weren't allowed to return to Venice unless we would adhere to the superstitions."

I wanted to roll my eyes because I could imagine two young boys not listening to that and taking it as a challenge instead. "I'm guessing their discipline had the opposite effect?"

His arm wrapped around my waist, and he drew me closer as we joined a group entering the piazza. "Of course." We wove through attendees garbed in elaborate and colorful costumes like ours as he guided us to our table. "We were forever getting into trouble."

After he pulled out my chair for me, I sat at our table, which was decorated with a cream tablecloth and gold accents. Pretty place cards were set around the table with our coinciding wine-charm numbers. Other tables were similar in design, but the highlighted colors matched the beads strung around their wine charms. It added to the evening's magic, and I was happy that we were a part of it.

Soft murmurs between people already seated, their masks firmly in place, complemented the mystery. I didn't know anyone, and if Sergio did, he wouldn't address them by name given the theme of the night.

My gaze darted around the piazza, taking in everything I could. An orchestra played Vivaldi's *Four Seasons* on one of the raised stands. There was space left open for dancing, and I hoped that Sergio would want to join the few who already circled the floor. Along the passerelle, attendants stood by shadow boxes that held auction items or easels with paintings also up for bid. Each employee matched one another, dressed in black and gold, appropriate colors for the event.

There was a possibility that we wouldn't be staying long, as Sergio was one of several experts on call for a complicated procedure set to take place first thing in the morning. As his reduced hours as a full-time surgeon was fairly recent, he was still called upon for consultations by the doctors in his former practice who now saw some of his former clients.

Sergio turned to respond to the husband and wife at his elbow, who had monopolized his attention for the past few minutes after he introduced me. They spoke of families in Rome I didn't know. I caught a glimpse of Daniela, who sent me a jaunty wave as a handsome man drew her into his arms on the dance floor.

When Adriano and David wove through the table and to my side, I sighed with relief to be free of the stuffy couple, leaving Sergio to extricate himself when he found the right opening.

Adriano held me at arm's length as his gaze took in the exquisite gown of his that I wore. I couldn't help an ear-to-ear grin from spreading across my face. "It's beautiful," I said with reverence.

"On you, it is."

David lightly slapped at Adriano's arm then motioned for his turn. When I turned to him, he enveloped me in a hug. "Stunning, Gianna."

I let loose a small nervous laugh at all the flattery. "You two are very dashing. My eye was drawn to you when we crossed the dance floor."

"Speaking of dancing"—Adriano leaned in—"when are you two going to?"

I rolled my eyes. "Soon, I would think. And what about the two of you? I don't see you out there."

"That's because we're here for the wine, food, and gossip." David gave a conspiratorial wink. "And to network," he said pointedly to Adriano.

"If you don't mind." Adriano ignored David, his attention focused on me. "I'd like to show you off to a few people, even though the dress isn't exactly a one of a kind."

A chill skated across my spine as it snapped straight. "What do you mean?" But I knew, even though I was loath to admit it out loud. Sophia had worn the very same frock more than a century ago. I felt her with me when Sergio was not physically touching me, along with a heavy sense of expectancy, both good and bad.

Adriano's brows furrowed as he brushed several of his braids over a shoulder. "I thought I told you this." At the shake of my head, his frown deepened. "I was rummaging through a box of old photographs and came across a few taken before going out to the Carnival sometime in the early 1900s. My dad identified one of the women as my aunt, but it was another woman who wore a dress almost identical to the one I made for you."

The orchestra reached a crescendo, and the music swelled over the dance floor, urging me to step away and join the dancers in a complicated waltz, far from the conversation taking place.

"Do you know who she was?" My pulse thundered in my ears, and a wave of dizziness swept over me. I remembered the bright bulb of the flash as Sophia descended the stairs. I didn't need Adriano to confirm that it was Sophia, but I still wanted to hear him say her name, to tether the vision I'd had into the present.

"She reminded me of you." David stepped closer, concern etched in the downturn of his lips. "Are you all right?"

I edged up to our table then reached for my wine. After a hearty gulp, I pasted a smile on my face and nodded despite the unease that trailed my every movement. "Of course. I'm fine." Another sip. "The picture. Who was in it?"

Wariness clouded Adriano's eyes. "When I asked Marco, he said he thought it was Sophia, a young woman who, at the time, was engaged to one of my nefarious relations."

"Nefarious?" Violently burying the terror at who I knew him to be, I could appreciate Adriano's term and attempt at levity.

David waved his hand between us. "Enough of this. We're at a party. There is an open bar, and I think we need something a bit stronger. Then we dance!" He looped my arm through his, Adriano took the other side, and with a brief explanation to Sergio, we were off in search of something stronger to sustain us after the topic we'd skirted around a moment ago.

For the next two hours, we chatted amongst ourselves and with our tablemates, enjoyed a delicious meal, and danced. All the weighty history surrounding the dress faded, and I enjoyed every minute of our evening.

Adriano and David stopping by our table added immensely to the evening's enjoyment. They were the ones who'd pulled us onto the dance floor before the first course and again immediately after dinner, and we stayed at the party for several hours. Not once did Sergio leave my side if Adriano and David weren't with me, and I was grateful.

Sergio bid on several paintings that caught our eye. They would find a home in his office in Rome if he won the auction. Partied out, I was relieved when Sergio suggested we return home, where the magic would continue. I was all for it.

When it was time to go, we said our goodbyes then made our way around the dance floor to the exit of the piazza. His hand slipped from mine as a man jogged up to have a quick word with him. After introductions, he extracted us from the short conversation, but the loss of his touch was already getting to me.

My breathing felt labored. The sense of being underwater, a spiraling panic, followed.

"What's wrong?" His voice was tight, as if he, too, struggled with the oppressive sensations.

Sergio's hand rested on my lower back, and I turned to him. "I don't know. I've been on edge here and there. Something with the piazza and the masquerade I think." *Or wearing the dress.*

He nodded. "I feel it too. Oddest thing, but it seems to go away when I'm touching you."

I allowed a small smile to curve my lips as I leaned into his side. "I agree. So don't let go."

His hand slipped around my waist, secure on my hip. I wound my arm around him, too, a sigh of contentment easing past my lips as the last remnants of the odd emotions evaporated.

The walk back went so much faster than getting to the party. Once we were inside the Marcello home, our goblets were deposited on a nearby surface, and we made our way upstairs. He lit several candles, and soon, soft lighting cast a warm glow around our room, where we both kicked off our shoes.

"Let me help you." His deep voice held a huskiness that heightened my desire, and our eyes locked, connecting us to what we would do together.

He stood close enough for me to breathe in his scent. With care, he removed my mask then the clip that fastened my hair. His fingers threaded through the strands, massaging my scalp. As he released it, his gaze followed the thick mass as it tumbled down my shoulders. He turned me so he could lower the zipper from the gown in slow, tantalizing increments. The brush of his fingers along my bare skin sent a shiver of desire coursing through me. The dress pooled at my feet, and I stepped from it and into his arms.

He groaned then reached for me. "All night, the thought of being parted from you has been driving me crazy. I want to go slow, but I'm not sure I can with you standing before me. One touch of your hand, and you bring me to my knees."

The touch from his fingers grazing over my cheek sent a shiver through me. I was lost at his words, feeling how they echoed inside of me. I would relish slow too.

I stilled his hands so that I could remove his jacket and shirt. I placed the belt and trousers on top of where I'd tossed his other articles of clothing. We made short work of everything that prevented skin-on-skin contact. He lifted me in his arms then lay me on our bed, where I welcomed the weight of his body over mine.

The faint strains of the orchestra still played in my mind

as he brushed his lips over mine. My blood heated, and my heart rate increased as he deepened the kiss. With Sergio, every time was like the first, but also as if we'd done a similar dance a million times. The connection between us was filled with history and enchantment. It was special and something I knew would always stand the test of time.

I curled my fingers in his thick dark hair, bringing my lips to his. As his mouth moved over mine, every nerve in my body felt electrified. His touch lured me into a sense of synchronicity that was seemingly written into our DNA.

When he broke the kiss, I gasped at the loss, but he had other ideas. My skin heated where he kissed and licked his way down, and I writhed beneath him, my back arching. With the first touch of his tongue at the apex of my thighs, my head rocked back, and a moan escaped my lips. His fingers joined the friction as he moved them deep inside, bringing me to unimaginable heights. When I cried out with release, he traveled back up my body, settling between my legs, his hard length pushing at my entrance.

Fire blazed in his eyes, accentuated by the candlelight, and my mind played tricks on me. In the wake of ecstasy, his features merged and combined into the man of my dreams, the one who'd searched for me through time but held me tightly in the present.

I trailed my fingers over each ridge and hollow of his back before settling on his trim waist, applying pressure on the taut flesh to urge him to fill me. With a growl, he lowered his head, and our tongues intertwined in a kiss. Then he was inside me, and I moaned again.

He held me in his arms as he brought us higher. And when my world shattered around me in a burst of intoxicating passion and light, he followed.

As our breathing regulated, he withdrew from me, and I felt the loss instantly. Shifting to the side, he pulled me with him, so his weight was no longer pressing me into the mattress. A grin curved his kissable lips, and I matched the smile, joy dancing through my sensitive and utterly relaxed body. Making love with him would never get old. I nuzzled into his arms, resting my head on his chest as he traced soothing circles on my back. Content, I wondered if sleep would come or if there was more this incredible night would bring.

The night wasn't over. It was late, but Sergio and I were both keyed up from the party and the hour we'd just spent in each other's arms. When the shrill ring of his phone disrupted our evening, I'd gotten out of bed with him, not wanting to go to sleep just yet. Garbed in a pair of yoga pants, T-shirt, and cardigan, I wandered through the kitchenette and got a glass of water for Sergio.

The comforting sound of his voice trailed from the living room, where he took the call from a colleague. I meandered through the third floor of the Marcello home so that I could see the lights as they reflected off the canal. Even though the sky was dark, it was a clear night, and stars above shone with a white-gold full moon.

Movement caught my eye, and I spotted Cat on her dock. She was sitting outside amidst the glow of candles, sipping a glass of wine. The flickering light added an unmistakable ambiance to the setting.

With no idea how long Sergio's call would be, I went out to accompany her. The elegant and well-balanced strains of

Mozart played from an open window. It was an intimate and cozy atmosphere, and I couldn't help a wistful smile from curving my lips at the thought of Sergio and me enjoying a similar setting in our small alcove later that night. That I planned to start early by sharing a glass of wine with Cat wouldn't bother him in the least.

Cat sat in the chair that faced the bridge and the Marcello residence. Her long silver hair fell in soft waves around her gracefully aging face and thin frail shoulders. She had a dark shawl wrapped around her to ward off the cool November air.

"Do you mind if I join you?" I hovered near an empty chair. The flowers lent an intoxicating scent even at night. A vase containing an artful array of exotic blossoms, probably the ones Sergio had brought her, sat on the table.

Cat's tired gaze rested on me, devoid of her usual lustrous shine, but she mustered an effort to chase it away with the hint of a smile that curved her lips. "I hoped you would."

"Are you all right?" I settled across from her and leaned on my elbows.

"Of course." There was a glass of red wine waiting, and she slid it in front of me. "It's one of those evenings where Lorenzo's presence is missed acutely." She paused to sip hers, and I did the same. "I can feel him here tonight, calling me to his side."

"Don't say that, Cat." Alarm sizzled across the exposed skin of my face and neck, and I covered her hand with mine. "Are you unwell?"

She returned the squeeze to my hand. "No, Bella. Just tired and a little encouraged that the time to reunite with my love is upon me."

"I—"

"Shh. It's not for you to worry over." She withdrew her

hand and took another small sip. "Have I ever told you the story of the sixteenth-century philosopher and mathematician, Giordano Bruno?"

"No, I can't remember you mentioning anything about him." I shivered as a chilly wind swept through the canal, ruffling the lush foliage on Cat's dock.

"Well, the story isn't what I want to get into tonight, only that his ghost occasionally appears to elderly women over the age of eighty-five, which my dear friend Maribel is. The other night when I went to dinner with friends, Maribel and I saw, in an upper window of Ca'Mocenigo, what had to have been Giordano's face engulfed in flames."

"Wait, I thought you were eighty-three."

"That's where the meaning behind the sighting is significant."

I worried my lower lip, the vision she painted an unpleasant one. "I can't imagine seeing Giordano's ghost in such a brutal manner. But it doesn't mean anything that you did. It's just one of those strange occurrences."

"What it indicates is that the veil is thinning between the living and the deceased for Maribel and me. After the sighting, we talked at length about our interpretation of why, and we've both made preparations, should we pass away unexpectedly."

"Cat, I—"

"Bella, don't worry about me. Passing from this world to the next isn't something I fear. Besides, my Lorenzo will be there with open arms."

A strange fuzziness came over my body, making my limbs feel languid and slow to respond to my cues. I squinted at the bottle on the table between us, unfamiliar with the Italian label. "Is this a new wine?"

Her watery eyes stole my breath. I was genuinely

concerned for her and hoped Sergio would be off his call soon to help. I didn't know if she needed medical attention or was just having a sad evening.

"This wine is from my wedding night. Lorenzo and I had a few bottles stashed away. We brought them out to enjoy on special occasions."

Things were finally making sense, and the tension between my shoulder blades eased. "Is it your anniversary?"

"Today would have been sixty-four years of celebrating the love of my life and our marriage. I would do anything to have him here with me again."

"I'm sure he is here with you in spirit, Cat."

"Yes." For a moment, pure joy erased years from her aging movie-star face. "Enough about me. Tell me how the masquerade was?"

"Well, it was an experience." I suppressed a shiver at the thought of how a sense of dread had trailed my every step, the tight grip Sergio had on me the majority of the time the only thing keeping a full-fledged panic attack at bay.

"That it is. The dress you wore, the one Adriano designed, reminds me so much of another, a picture I once saw in the Delluccis' home. I hadn't wrapped my mind around who, with absolute certainty, until I saw you in it."

"Really? Adriano told me that while he was making it, the experience had been almost trancelike, and he had found a picture as inspiration for the gown. Not only that, but every time he tried to put the dress in the main showroom for sale, something stopped him."

"Until you." Her voice warbled a little at the end.

"Yes." It was unusual, but I couldn't very well complain. The design was perfect, and when I'd slipped it on even that very first time, it was as if it was made for me. While in it, I'd felt as though I'd worn the gown before, and at the beginning of the evening, it lent a certain vitality and magic.

"In truth, it was made for you, and there's a reason behind it. But before I get into all that, I want to tell you about a dear friend of mine."

I melted back in my chair to listen, lulled by the sound of her voice and the weightiness of my limbs. I suppressed a yawn behind my hand, unsure of where the sudden tiredness had come from.

With the stem of her glass, Cat twirled her wine several times. In the flickering candlelight and the moon's glow, I could see the legs of red drag down the sides of her goblet. "I was heartbroken when Lorenzo died just shy of forty years ago."

The sound of her voice held me captive. The gentle ripple of the canal after a lantern-lit gondola sailed by with two lovers wrapped arm in arm added to the story's intimacy, and I took small sips of wine while listening.

"I was devastated when the heart attack took him from me. After the first week, my friends dragged me out of the house, and we spent many hours here on this very dock." She swept her hand around her outdoor area. "When it came time for them to go home, I often stayed outside a while longer. At the time, it was a common occurrence to experience the scent of plaster and paint permeating the space between the Marcello residence and ours."

I'd heard a little about that from Francesca Marcello. It was believed that the inconsolable artist returned under the light of the moon to touch up any damage on the fresco mural.

"Then one evening"—Cat's wistful sigh carried the weight of years—"he appeared."

"Who appeared?"

"Giovanni." She lifted a shaky hand as she pointed to the alley between her home and the Marcellos' and to the fresco. I held my breath. "He comforted me in ways I can never fully express. The ones we loved, my husband, his Sophia, was so profound that it spanned time. Still, he searched for his Sophia, swearing to find her again someday. It gave me such hope that my Lorenzo and I would reunite too."

"Do you think that was why he never moved on? Why he hadn't been able to reunite with Sophia beyond the grave?"

Her gaze drifted back toward the finished fresco. "He had unfinished business here that I suspect kept him tethered… the fresco and how Sophia's last moments were spent."

I wanted to comfort her, but it was getting hard to keep my eyes open. I was so sleepy.

"But everything has changed. You've made that possible. When I saw you in the gown that Adriano was compelled to make, I knew what I would have to do. You've returned, Sophia, and I can help you find your way back to Giovanni. We'll go together."

I commanded my eyelids to open wide, taking in the softly flickering candlelight to the shadows that danced over her features. "I don't understand."

"As I've told you, the veil is thinning for me, Bella. It's time I return to my Lorenzo. It's the way I want to go. After I saw you wearing the masquerade gown, I knew without a shadow of a doubt that you'd returned. You, my sweet Sophia, will join me. Giovanni is waiting for you too."

With effort, Cat gained her feet then came to stand before me. Her hands reached for mine. Confusion swirled, and the weird dreams and déjà vu started to seem more real. I longed for Giovanni. The feeling was ingrained deep in my soul. I glanced again at Cat's outstretched hand and placed mine in hers. My mind swirled, and I had trouble separating the present from the past visions and dreams I'd experienced. If she could take me to Giovanni, then I would follow her.

I wobbled on unsteady legs, clinging to her frail, bony

hand. My feet moved as if I was floating as Cat and I left her dock. Her hand tightened, and she led me to the ledge, where warnings whispered with the wind. We tiptoed along the narrow lip of the Marcello home, where a gondola would stop for entrance into my favorite alcove and watery entrance. But there wasn't a gondola there, just the waiting arms of the placid water before us.

We remained there, time suspended, and I mirrored how Cat's foot hovered over the canal. Everything was foggy in my mind. What she'd said was hard to discern from reality. We were going to see Giovanni. I would follow her lead. I trusted her, and the tinge of danger faded in the wake of the intoxicating relaxation that had plagued my entire body since the first few sips of wine.

"It's time." A wistful longing laced Cat's words, and I readied myself to go with her. A slight shuffle sounded, and I followed the sound. My murky gaze strayed to the bridge, where a blurry figure stood. There was something oddly familiar about the shape of the person and the hood that concealed their features from me. A shiver danced over my body, one not derived from the chilly evening air.

Cat's hand tightened on mine, and I let the image on the bridge fade in place of who we would soon see. It'd been so long since I'd heard Giovanni's voice and lost myself in his all-consuming obsidian gaze. But the promise between us still stood. We belonged together. I wanted to go to him, just as much as she did to her Lorenzo.

"Come, Bella. They're waiting." Her voice warbled, heavy with exhaustion and unmistakable longing.

A slight tug from Cat, and we were going. A shiver of anticipation spread through my lethargic limbs. At the giddy peep from Cat, I couldn't help but turn to see the mirrored faraway expression of excitement on her features, which matched my own anticipation of the embrace we both sought. Our bodies tilted forward as one, and a sliver of worry over what we were doing attempted to gain a stronghold, but the fuzziness that ruled my mind shushed it. They would catch us. We would be okay.

"No. Cat, stop."

The sharp command sent a volley of shock through my system. I jolted back a little, dragging Cat with me. Some of the fuzziness dissipated. I jerked my foot back, my sluggish heart kicking up a notch, helping to push back another layer of confusion. Horror followed swiftly in its wake. *What are we doing?*

Cat's hand slipped from mine, and my sleepy gaze tracked her as the peaceful smile that had graced her face slipped away at the interruption. The voice was familiar, but the shock over my confused state and willingness to drown with Cat to reunite with Giovanni sent tremors throughout my body. I withdrew my extended foot, placing it securely on the ledge, tugging at Cat to do the same. A firm grip on my arm anchored me along with Cat as the woman pulled us back. I turned my head as I followed to see who it was. "Francesca."

"I'm sorry, Gianna." Sorrow pulled her features taut. "I tried to call and also to get here earlier, but the water taxi was delayed. There was something wrong with my phone. The texts and calls seemed to go through, but I don't think any of them did."

What does she mean by that? "How did you know?" I slipped an arm around a visibly shaken Cat, who had tears streaming down her anguished face.

Francesca grimaced. "I didn't know for sure that this would happen. I had a dream last night that I couldn't ignore. I knew it was time to come home."

"He was waiting for me, Frannie. Now he's gone," Cat

wailed, and my heart broke for the older woman despite what she'd attempted to do.

I still felt the aftereffects of the wine. There had been something in it—I was sure of it. There was no other reason why I would have followed her lead so docilely. Still, it affected my thought process and my motor skills. I had to focus hard to keep my arm around Cat, to help Francesca lead her to her back door.

"I can stay with her tonight." Francesca looked at me over Cat's head. Behind her trendy tortoiseshell glasses, her brown eyes swam with tears. Her chin-length hair, normally immaculate and shinny, was a disheveled mop. She appeared to be as rattled as I was. "Are you sure you're all right?"

"I'm feeling much better. Promise."

Francesca seemed torn, but the sob that tumbled from Cat distracted her. "Is Sergio inside?"

"Yes," I managed.

"Good. Go right in and get some rest. I'll check in with you tomorrow." Francesca guided Cat back to her deck and opened the door to the home. But they didn't close the door. Instead, they hovered just inside, talking in hushed whispers.

Worry over Cat's mental state made it hard for me to leave, but I did as Francesca said and turned on an unsteady heel. I left Cat's dock and was about to head to the Marcello manor's door, where Sergio was just inside and on his conference call, when I heard another shuffle to my right.

Fear licked up my spine at the realization that I'd forgotten about the cloaked figure on the bridge. The very same one that had filled my peripheral vision was no longer on the bridge but at my elbow.

"Why are you still here?" a woman's voice hissed with unmistakable fury.

I knew the owner of that voice. "Lucia?"

When I turned, I was met with a menacing sneer, and I

took a step back. My skin crawled, as it often did in her presence—I carried a deep-set fear of her that I couldn't explain. In a slow perusal, I took in the cloak around her shoulders and the hood that concealed her face. Standing directly in front of her, though, meant I could see her.

No. It was a confrontation that I didn't need. The sight of her cloak worried me even more, especially given when I'd seen it last. I jerked my gaze to her hand. On her finger was the oversized diamond flanked by rubies that had caught the moonlight the night I'd witnessed Antoinette's death. My foggy mind pieced together that that had been a warning from beyond the grave, one I wish I'd confronted Lucia about in the presence of others, because I was not in a good scenario.

Her finger jammed into my shoulder, and I was forced to take an unsteady step back. I had to know for sure and couldn't stop myself from confronting her. "You were the one on the bridge the night Antoinette died. You killed her."

With her lips pulled back in an angry sneer, she leaned close. "The foolish woman tried to take what's mine. But I wasn't going to let her have it."

"Marco?" I couldn't understand why she'd called him "it."

"He was a tool to get what I deserved, what I'd always wanted. The house, status, and of course the money. It was all mine, and there was no way I would let some interloper steal even a cent from under me. I'd worked too hard to establish the life I wanted. I even had a child with that man."

I couldn't wrap my brain around what she was talking about or why she would say those things. I'd seen her with Daniela. Maybe motherhood wasn't what she'd originally wanted, but she loved her daughter. As for Marco, I'd never seen the two of them together beyond that one time on their balcony. But he had been reading the paper. As far as I could tell, they weren't communicating.

But to kill someone for a loveless life like what she had…
I couldn't understand the reasons behind it. She was sick. I
hadn't told Adriano about her or what I'd witnessed her do
to his mother, but maybe I should have. The problem was, I
still didn't have proof. It would be her word against mine.

She forced me back another step, her fingers digging
into my shoulder. There would be a bruise. My heel landed
without anything solid beneath it, and I realized that I stood
at the edge of the ledge, close to where Cat and I had been
just moments before. Taking that final plunge would have
been insane, and I still struggled with how readily I'd
agreed, but it would have been peaceful. What was
happening with Lucia was nothing like that. The menacing
glint in her eyes, visible by the glow of the lamp at the end
of the bridge, told me what was in her heart. Death. She
meant for me to die, and there were no witnesses to see her
true evil.

It was a guess, but I had to know. "You convinced Cat that
she and I would meet her husband and Giovanni tonight."

"Very good." The sneer morphed into a cold smile. "It was
easy. She always struggles on her anniversary. She just needs
a nudge here and there. I stopped by as soon as she came
outside this evening. When I poured a glass of wine and
slipped the belladonna in it, I easily extracted myself and told
her that since I hadn't had any, she should save it for you. I
laid the groundwork by showing an old picture. Then I made
the connection of who you really are and told Cat, something she saw with her own eyes tonight."

"And who is that?" I needed to hear her say it.

"Sophia, of course. You see, I recognized your last name."

"Bellini?"

She snorted. "No. Your mother's last name."

"I never told you her name."

"Pff. That was easy to find out. I did a little research and learned your mother's maiden name is Capozzi. That's the same line that Sophia is from. *You're her.*"

While I agreed that there was a connection, it wouldn't have been to Sophia. Lucia was crazy. "Just because we share a common surname doesn't mean I'm her. And even if I was Sophia reincarnated, why is that important to you?"

"Because you don't belong here. And my Daniela will have the security and status that Sergio can provide."

I opened my mouth to argue, but the words never materialized. With a hard shove from Lucia, I flew backward. Francesca's cry pierced the air, a lifeline that had no substance to save me.

With a splash, water enveloped me. One minute, I was standing in the cool night air, and in the next, I was below the water's surface. No amount of pleading and fighting with my sluggish limbs made any difference. I was still drugged and sank into the murky canal's depths.

Shafts of light beckoned from the homes and the lamps on the ends of the bridge above as I drifted far below the surface. Awareness trickled in, and the stirrings of panic swirled in my mind.

My lungs fought the immense pressure of the water, but it won. I swallowed one gasping mouthful after another while my limbs refused to answer my call to work, to climb to the fading light that beckoned along the surface above.

I won't be saved. I won't be found.

Time and space lost meaning as I floated down, my life fading. Bubbles slipped from my nose and lips, and my long dark hair billowed around me, obscuring the lights shinning above the surface as I sank farther.

Everything stilled. I felt a tug. My descent stopped. There was a flash of white as ghostly fingers curled around my wrist. *Giovanni.* He pulled. My eyelids drooped.

From a distance, I heard a splash and a ripple of disturbance in the water around me. The pressure on my lungs faded as my dreamlike vision below the surface blurred. The grasp around my wrist tightened, and everything faded.

A dark void engulfed me. Then there was nothing.

A ball of light blinded me, and a wave of peace soon followed. I found myself floating, suspended in Giovanni's embrace. When I turned in his arms, the canal's chill faded until it was nonexistent. I feasted on the sight of those gray eyes that I'd known from when we'd first met, the very same that haunted my dreams as well as my first night lost in the fog in Venice. He'd called to me throughout the years until I'd returned to where I was meant to be. I luxuriated in his strength, the watery grave replaced by another time where I recalled the familiar masculine scent that was uniquely his. As he bent his head to accommodate my smaller stature, I brushed a lock of dark hair from his forehead. To touch him again… it was everything.

Pulses of pressure bloomed through my chest, distracting me from Giovanni. When I looked down from where I was, held secure in Giovanni's arms, I saw paramedics working tirelessly on my body until a burst of water was expelled from my lungs, clearing the way for stuttered gasps of air.

The duality of my situation lanced me with pain. My corporeal eyes remained closed. Giovanni left for a time. I was alone, floating above my body. Not long after, I could sense Sergio's pleas as he begged me to stay with him, to wake up. The need to return to him was unrelenting and urgent.

Activity buzzed around my physical body. Tethered to it I remained devoid of pain and discomfort. Time passed differently.

In an altered form, floating above all that happened on the pavement near the canal, I couldn't feel Sergio, and I was desperate to. The more I longed to be with him, the clearer his palpable despair became as it traveled through a thin silver cord that seemed to link us and shook me to my core. I watched as he held my physical body in his arms, keeping me safe and warm. It wasn't long until a water taxi approached. He stood, never letting me go.

The scene below faded and I wasn't sure how much time passed. Eventually, Giovanni reappeared, taking my hand in his. I wanted Sergio, but couldn't see him. I didn't know where he was.

I inched away from Giovanni's hold, torn between Sophia's life and my own. The century might have been different, but the depth of love wasn't.

Not even time could keep us apart

"A few minutes more, Sophia, please." Giovanni's deep voice lassoed me back, and I focused solely on him, knowing Sergio would keep my physical body safe and that until it was time to return, Giovanni would do the same for my spirit.

I rested my hand along the angle of Giovanni's jaw, the memory of the festival haunting me as Sophia's memories solidified as my own. The horror was still fresh over how Edoardo had found and detained me, keeping me from leaving with Giovanni. I sighed into his embrace. "I knew you would come for me."

"I promised you we would be together again." His deep voice reverberated through his chest and into mine. "The memories, the dreams and visions, were meant for more than a remembrance. They were a warning that we weren't the only ones who'd returned. Edoardo... he chose to inter-vene once again."

"But he's gone. He can't hurt me anymore." I was confused. "Where was Edoardo?" The touch of Giovanni's hand against my cheek chased the worry away, and I focused fully on him.

Ours was a rebellion against time, and our stolen moments were coming to an end. I sensed the tether to my physical body pulling me away.

He threaded his fingers through my hair, and his eyes darkened from gray to obsidian.

When his gaze flicked to the scene below us, I was helpless to follow. Somehow, we were closer, suspended over a woman lying in a hospital bed that Sergio sat beside. His he held her hand even while asleep and slumped over in his chair. Hours must have passed, if not days. His clothes were rumbled and a dusting of hair covered his face. He needed to shave again.

The soft beep of a machine monitored her heartbeat, while she lay tucked under stark-white covers. Long dark hair spilled over the pillow. I observed from above, hovering in Giovanni's arms and not fully registering the body as my own but watching how her face angled toward the protective man hovering beside her. Despite the intertwined memories of the life I'd lived with Giovanni in the past, I still recognized myself.

"It's time to go back, Sophia." His voice rumbled through his chest in a mixture of desperation and longing that mirrored the emotions raging through me as well.

A tremor ran through my body at the thought of experiencing the trauma of drowning. He tangled his fingers in my hair, cupping the back of my head then nudging me to observe the scene below us once more. "We have a second chance."

All the dreams, the familiarity of Venice's labyrinth streets, the various moments where I felt ill—when Sophia had brushes with fate, with death—they all made sense, as did the recognition, the instant pull I'd experienced upon meeting Sergio and how he'd been unable to leave Venice, or that café, the day we'd met.

Giovanni was right. We had another chance. Returning would be the chance we had been denied.

We were fated to reunite.

He held my hand, guiding me to merge with the prone form below. It was time. With one last nudge, I left Giovanni's arms.

The following afternoon, after returning from the hospital, Sergio and I sat on the couch and talked for hours. He believed me about Giovanni. Even so, there were questions. We thought their spirits had influenced our meeting, but we hadn't said the words I knew to be true.

Instead, I looked at our time as the gift it was—another chance. We didn't need to muddy the path forward by focusing on the past. We would forge a new way, and I would enjoy every step of it.

Sergio had Lucia arrested, having witnessed her shoving me into the canal, and belladonna had been found in the blood test Sergio ordered for me. Between that and giving a statement to a detective who visited me during my short stay in the hospital, they had plenty of evidence to put her away. Cat and Francesca also recounted the parts of the evening they'd witnessed.

Pushing those thoughts aside, I focused on being fully present with Sergio, and a soft smile curved my lips as happiness filled every fiber of my being.

As we'd done on many evenings together, we enjoyed the

night air while sipping wine at the small table in our alcove. Reflections from the buildings around us splashed across the small swells of the canal as if on a colorful canvas, broken only by the silent gondolas slipping by.

I stood from the small table and studied the alcove's fresco painting. The mural had weathered surprisingly well for its age and location. When I'd first asked Francesca about it, she'd said no repairs were needed just yet—in time, yes, but not until the summer.

"Everything okay?"

Sergio's deep baritone surprised me while I was lost in thought. My gaze traced the frothy whitecaps in the painting to where the sun sparkled off one particular area more than the rest. There was an indentation at the top, and cracks had formed around what appeared to be a cinderblock shape. It was very odd. I'd noticed it before but was suddenly unable to let it go.

"Yes," I murmured in response to his question. I pointed at the mural. "It appears as if a repair occurred at some point." *A bad one?*

"That's intentional. It's one of Il Verrocchio's secrets."

Giovanni's secrets. I still couldn't recall all of the memories from Sophia's time with him a century before, and maybe that was best. It would allow me to live in the moment, not the past.

"Come and see." He set the wineglasses on the small table before fitting his fingers into the slight indentation. With a tug, the cut portion of the wall swung out, opening like a small door.

I crowded him, excitement sizzling through my blood. "Do you know what's inside?"

He reached in. "I do. I discovered it years ago. It's something my aunt claimed she knew nothing about." The wink told me he didn't believe her for a second.

"Did you show her?"

He withdrew a wooden box about the size of my hand. "I did, but she told me to put it back, that it wasn't time."

My gaze jerked back to him. "She told me the same thing about restoring this painting."

A mischievous grin curved his face as he put the box away then indicated I should have a seat. "I'm beginning to understand more and more why she says the things she does."

There did seem to be a pattern to her comments. Her suggestion to change his work hours was one example. As for the rest, I hoped time would tell.

My gaze strayed across to the Delucci home and the balcony where I'd once spotted Edoardo through Sophia's eyes. "I hope Edoardo paid for his crime."

"He did not. There were no witnesses aside from her lover, who was deemed unreliable due to the scandalous nature of their affair."

"Like Lucia."

He nodded his agreement. "But she's paying for her crimes against you. Maybe not for Antoinette, as we don't have proof, but the charges against her will stick."

I was glad she was behind bars, but I wished Daniela and Adriano didn't have to bear the weight of what she had done. It was a bitter pill to swallow, and I knew they felt terrible, given their obvious remorse when they'd visited me in the hospital. But we would all get through it.

Could that be what Giovanni had meant? That Edoardo was here, too, but with an unrecognizable face? "It's weird, but I keep thinking of her as a modern-day Edoardo."

Distaste crossed his features, and he threaded his fingers through mine, pulling me close. "I could easily believe that to be true."

At his urging, I shifted from my seat to his lap, where he wound his arms around me. Still, I couldn't let Giovanni's and Sophia's endings go. "Do you know how it happened? How Sophia's fiancé found out about her and Giovanni?"

His fingers played with the ends of my hair. "It was late at night, and she'd slipped away to meet Giovanni. Edoardo somehow discovered them together and followed her the night of the masquerade, intercepting Sophia before she could unite with her lover. From what I know, Giovanni dived in and tried to save her. He was not able to find her. There was no body to recover."

Tears rolled down my cheeks. My body broke out in chills, the story resonating in my soul. "The canals aren't deep, are they?"

"In some places, yes. There is an area near where she fell in that drops to thirty or sixty feet. Heartbroken, Giovanni turned to drink then took his own life."

We leaned against one another, each needing the comfort. As the story eased from our immediate thoughts, Sergio stood. My legs slid down his body, and he clasped my hand then took me with him to the section of the mural with the secret door, where he removed the box from its hiding place. A perplexed frown marred his handsome features as he turned it over in his hands.

I leaned close, fascinated with the story and the box he held. "Do you think there is more for us to discover about Giovanni and Sophia?" The way he studied the wood sent an expectant thrill racing along my skin. I wanted to know everything about their story, the parts I couldn't recall.

There were unmistakable urges to seek the truth, to put the past fully to rest. Together, I hoped that Sergio and I could do that. I suspected I wouldn't see Giovanni again except for when I gazed upon my Sergio. Although their noses were different—Sergio's was a tad crooked—there were similarities in the shape of their faces, their firm jaws, and their seductive eyes.

"The notes they'd left for one another. I don't know... I've always believed there would be more... a last letter from Sophia or maybe even Giovanni." Sergio turned the box this way and that, pressing on it. He pushed on the side.

"What is it?"

A grin curved his mouth, and I leaned forward for a better look. After lifting the lid, he pushed the side panel again.

It slid open to reveal a folded piece of aged paper nestled in a small drawer. With care, Sergio removed it. "This is Giovanni's handwriting." Awe filled his voice.

I scooted closer while he translated the letter to English as he read it aloud.

My Sweet Sophia,

My final words to you, my love, will be written here—until we meet again. The first moment I saw you walking across the bridge, life made sense. I thought I'd been happy before. But my life hadn't been complete, not until the moment our gazes collided. Our souls recognized one another.

I know we spoke of it a time or two, but I believe we will have another chance and that this tragic lifetime was not our first. I'm not far behind you. Our time will come again.

I'll search for you, Sophia, always.

When I learned of your engagement, I wanted to tear you from Edoardo's side. He was volatile and derisive. I denied you belonged to another or that the radiant creature walking with him was to be his new bride.

If only I'd known our fate ahead of time... I'd have taken you far from Venice's magical shores. Alas, I did not.

I cherish every note you left for me in our grotto. We will always have those moments. As I write to you, my fingers itch to caress your silky skin and to trail along the gentle curve of your cheek, and my lips long to brush against the heaven of you.

I would give anything to hold you in my arms again. I'm leaving this world. I cannot live another day without you. I've lost the will to paint. The final panel of our mural sits bare. One day, we will return, and it will be complete. I will forever remember the night I held you before the gods and we partook of the fountain's promise.

The beach—that was our downfall. It seemed harmless enough. Your note that Edoardo would be leaving that very day to attend business fed us false expectations. He must have seen us walking the Lido shoreline, staying just out of reach of the Adriatic Sea's playful froth. Those hours in the sun with you by my side will have to sustain me. They were the last.

That evening, during the weeks of Carnevale di Venezia, will forever haunt my soul. I searched for you and would have recognized you anywhere, mask or no mask. You weren't there.

I wish I could say this to you, talk to you, and touch you once more. This letter will have to suffice. I need to explain, even if only in the written word, what happened those last hours.

I went to our café, knowing I would find you there since you were not amidst the crowd in the cobbled streets. I didn't expect him.

I was too late. Those moments will forever stain my soul—you pleaded with that monster as he raged.

My God, Sophia. I died a thousand deaths when he shoved you. I rushed forward, but it was too late. You'd flown backward, your head striking the tethered gondola. Blood marred the edge of the vessel, and you plummeted into the arms of the sea. I searched for you. I didn't want you to die alone. I tried to follow you. Nothing else mattered.

That particular span of the canal ran far deeper than I could dive, and I couldn't have sustained consciousness under the freezing *water. My fight for life, even as I write these last words to you, is ebbing.*

It's time. I cannot survive another moment in this world until we can walk it together again, freely and hand in hand. For now, I will succumb to the arms of the ocean if that is the only way to be close to you. Until the next lifetime, my love.

Yours in life and death,

Giovanni

I CHOKED BACK my tears and squeezed Sergio's hand tighter. I met his gaze. A sheen of mist coated his deep-brown eyes. My heart could not have broken or soared any more than it did in that moment.

We'd found one another again. I had no doubt. In this life, we were meant to be together.

wo months later...

I STOOD in the living room, gazing out the windows as the sun's descent cast long shadows from the surrounding homes and bridges. Sergio was in the kitchen putting together cicchetti and wine for us to enjoy on the small alcove that opened to the canal. It was, and I suspected always would be, a favorite place of ours.

That afternoon, I'd spent hours with Cat and Francesca on Cat's dock. All had been forgiven regarding the incident where she'd attempted to reunite me with Giovanni. The love she'd had with her deceased husband was as strong as what Sophia and Giovanni had—and what Sergio and I experienced. Plus, she hadn't been in her right mind at the time, thanks to Lucia.

My fingers curled around the curtain that hung on the side of the floor-to-ceiling window as I leaned against the pane, watching as a gondola sailed by. My gaze flicked to the

Dellucci residence and Daniela, Adriano, David, and Marco enjoying dinner on their second-story terrace. My heart was heavy for them but also thankful that they didn't hold me accountable for Lucia's actions.

One evening, with Sergio by my side, I told Adriano a halting rendition of the crime Lucia had committed against his mother. I still don't know if it was the right decision, but with his family surrounding him, I was sure he'd come to terms with the news. Lucia's guilt firmly rested on her shoulders, and they'd all professed their sadness about what she'd put me through and what she'd put Adriano and Marco through. Deep inside, I was glad justice had been served, as she would pay for what she had done.

With Francesca's return and the buon fresco I was hired to restore and complete done, she'd involved me in the nonprofit organization to restore and repair Venice's artwork. In addition, she and Sergio had insisted I use Giovanni's fourth-floor residence as my art studio, as he had done when he was alive and living there.

Sergio and I lived together on the third floor and traveled to Rome when the need arose because of his work. I didn't always accompany him, but if I was able to step away from my art, there was no place I would rather be than by his side. He was loath to part from me, as well, and had made arrangements to access remotely as many of his meetings with the board as he could.

His aunt maintained the second floor as a residence for when she would eventually return to live there. But that wouldn't be for several years, as Cat was doing better, and the companionship with Francesca was a blessing.

Warmth settled against my back as Sergio pressed against me, slipping his arms around my waist. "Did you have a good visit with Francesca and Cat?"

Cat had been victimized by Lucia, and neither of us held

her responsible for her part in that night. I shifted in his arms and rose onto my toes so that I could brush a kiss across his lips. Dropping back to my heels, I smiled. "I did. She's doing much better, especially since Francesca moved in. I think the loneliness was getting to be too much for her."

"I spoke with Aunt Francesca this morning, and she is taking Cat on a cruise. She thought it would be good for her to get away for a little while."

His arms slid away, but he captured my hand in his. As I stepped away from the window, he lifted the platter with the cicchetti in his free hand. Wanting to help, I released my hold on him and picked up the bottle of wine and glasses. "Ready?"

Sergio grinned, and I tilted my head at the nervous energy in his hurried movements to usher us to the alcove. I laughed and looked behind me at his hovering form. After slipping through the doorway and setting our food and drinks at the table, he drew me into his arms for a toe-curling kiss. I didn't want it to end, but when he stepped back and pulled out my chair, I settled into it. Something was going on, and I hoped he would clue me in soon.

When he went to the secret compartment nestled in the mural's wall, my spine straightened, and my skin sizzled. "Did you find something else?"

"Not exactly." He removed the box that Giovanni and Sophia had left messages in to communicate to one another then set it on the table between us. "There is another small compartment I didn't show you but one I've planned to reveal since the day we first met. I knew even then what we would have together."

With care, he lifted the lid. A ring was nestled amidst what looked like dry baby-rosebud potpourri, and I sucked in a breath. He held the vintage oval-cut halo ring between us. The bloodred ruby sparkled. He turned the ring between his fingers. "This was meant for her, his true love. He had it made."

My gaze dropped back to the ring. "It's beautiful."

"Aunt Francesca passed the ring to me, and I believe Giovanni would have wanted us to have it."

My heart pounded as Sergio dropped to a knee before me. I was vaguely aware of a flash of movement as a gondola silently glided by the opening to our private patio. Then everything faded except the handsome man on his knee before me.

"Gianna, I've waited my entire life for you. When you arrived in the gondola, I knew that you were the one. It's been crazy, a whirlwind romance. We've only known each other for a couple of months, but it feels like a lifetime and then some. We are destined for one another. You're my soul mate."

Tears ran in rivers down my cheeks. *Is this happening?* With the same certainty that I'd been to Venice in another lifetime, I knew we were destined for one another. He touched the side of my face, and I smiled through my happy tears.

"Without you, I'm incomplete. I want to spend a lifetime and then some making you happy. Will you do me the honor of being my wife?"

Oh god, I... there were no words. Joy exploded through my body. I whispered "yes," and the final puzzle piece clicked into place as he slid the ring onto my finger. Warmth danced along my skin, and I thought someone else hovered over my shoulder. Sergio surged to his feet and wrapped me in his arms. Laughing, I leaned back and had to blink the tears of happiness from my eyes.

The moment was one that would forever be etched in my mind. We were where we should be, and I would enjoy every wonderful moment with Sergio by my side.

He owes her his life.
She knows better.

One encounter with her surveillance target was all it took to change the course of Nadia Bennett's life. It was a once in a lifetime kind of connection and worth the risk—even if the price of saving him was to leave him behind and start anew.

When an underwater angel saves Cade Malone from a car accident, he fears he won't find her again. Years pass, but he's still unable to erase her from his thoughts, so he vows that the next time they meet, he won't let her slip away.

Under the moonlit sky, their paths cross, and the lines of demarcation blur as Nadia takes a chance at love even though a dark secret from her past could destroy their relationship.

Moonlit Mirage (A Cook Islands Romance) is now available.

CLICK HERE to get your copy and continue reading today!
https://amymckinleyauthor.com/moonlit-destination-series/

Cade

A LOUD CRACK sent a shot of adrenaline through me as a vehicle swerved into my lane. My hands tightened into a death grip on the steering wheel. There was no movement to my car, no change in how it drove. It must have been a rock from the other car's tire. Rather than risk an accident, I eased off the accelerator while crossing the bridge. The surge of energy slowly dissipated, and I again fought to stay alert.

"Rise Against" by Savior blared from my speakers, and I tapped my finger against the steering wheel to the beat. With a slow blink, I took my gaze from the road for a split second and lowered the windows to let in more of the cool August air, which I hoped would help me remain awake. It had been hot as hell during the day, but by nearly midnight, the temperature had dropped to a chilly sixty degrees. I was glad for it.

Despite my intentions to leave at a reasonable hour, I'd

stayed at my dad's company to finish some extra work for my grad-school internship, which meant I'd fulfilled my requirement. It was a relief, but all I wanted was to fall into bed and sleep for hours.

After the bridge—and I was almost at the end—I wouldn't have much farther to drive to get home.

Light glared in my rearview mirror from an oncoming car. Averting my eyes, I concentrated on the road, staying in my lane. They were coming fast. The bridge had two lanes bound to Long Island, and I was going slowly enough that they could go around me.

Chills swept down my spine and along my arms, awakening a sixth sense of some sort, and I glanced again in my rearview mirror. *Shit.* The car was flying, barreling down on me. I punched the accelerator. It didn't look like they were going to change lanes. Sweat broke out on my forehead as they rode my bumper. My grip tightened on the wheel. *Come on, pass me.* I was going seventy miles per hour. *If they hit me...*

Their turning signal went on, and I almost sagged in relief. They were going around. *Goddamn.* That scared the hell out of me. I was suddenly wide awake.

I maintained my speed. I heard the roar of their engine as they punched the accelerator. *Whoever that is must be drunk.* My gaze switched from my mirror to the road in front of me.

The car shifted to the left, leaving my lane. My grip on the wheel didn't ease. There was nowhere else to go, and it was too late for me to switch lanes with them straddling both. The guardrail was on my right. *Come on.* With excruciating slowness, they inched partially into the next lane, far too close. I pushed the accelerator down, giving them more room to get over.

The blinding light in my mirror eased, and a minuscule amount of tension left me. I could see them inching to my left from my side mirror. I kept up my speed, so close to the bridge's exit. Once the other car moved over, I would ease off the pedal, but not yet.

Metal crunched in a cringe-worthy explosion. The world spun as the wheel jerked in my hands. Pain lanced across my chest as the seat belt bit into me and locked tightly. Tires squealed. My head crashed into something. I fought for control. The car spun anyway. My vision tunneled at what was ahead. There was nothing I could do. The car slammed into the guardrail, and the airbag deployed only to deflate with a hiss. *Shit, the rails*—they couldn't withstand the impact of a car going this fast. *Please hold.*

It didn't.

I was trapped, held in place by the seat belt, staring out the side window. Then the car tipped. My stomach dropped with the car as it fell. I could only watch in horror as the car rushed toward the East River.

The impact of hitting the water was like a second car accident. It sounded almost like an explosion as the car collided with the river. Water instantly poured through the tops of the windows as darkness smothered my vision. I felt warm liquid trickle over my eye as the car slowly sunk. My heart was beating a million times faster than it should have been. With my right hand, I struggled with the seat belt. *Do not panic.*

It was stuck.

Water flooded into the car from the partially lowered windows. I was screwed. I didn't think the car that hit me had stopped. No one was coming. So late at night, the traffic wasn't heavy. I clicked on the overhead lights as a biting cold lapped at my knees.

Someone will stop. I had to believe it. The car kept sinking, and I struggled. With more room, I pushed at the seatbelt button then yanked on the strap as hard as I could. *Who made these things?* It didn't budge. I fought with it while gasping for breath. The water was at my chin and climbing. I took a deep breath then ducked underneath the surface, searching for anything to cut the belt away.

I wouldn't last much longer once the car was fully submerged. I tipped my head back, elongating my spine. My lips cleared the waterline but barely. I took in as much air as I could. My lungs burned as I yanked hard on the belt, but nothing happened.

Movement on my side of the car spiked a thread of hope, and I turned my head in that direction. The light from one of my headlights illuminated someone swimming toward me. I squinted through the inky darkness. It was a woman—no, a girl, maybe. She was small. As she neared, her dark hair billowed around her heart-shaped face. Her forehead creased, and I tugged at the belt so she would understand that I was stuck. My lungs burned. A small burst of air bubbled from my lips. *Am I hallucinating?*

This is it. I couldn't hold my breath much longer.

She positioned herself with her hands on the door handle and one foot on the side. Then she kicked the half window of glass. Her heel made contact with a clink of something metal, and glass shattered and floated around us. Not wasting a second, she reached inside and manually slid the lock to open. My mind was chaos. More air slipped past my lips. She gave a hard tug, but the door stayed shut. I tried too. Nothing happened.

She left my sight. I strained to see where she went. *Please don't leave!* But I didn't want her to die down there too. The car stopped sinking when the front end hit the river's murky bottom.

When she reappeared, the last of the air I'd been able to hold escaped. Half her body fit through the open window. I went to gasp, but she grabbed the back of my neck and then fit her lips over mine, like a seal. I fought to stay calm. She shoved her tongue in my mouth, and tiny zaps of electricity exploded through my body at her touch. There were worse ways to die. I went with it.

My eyelids drifted shut, and I let myself feel her softness. My fingers ached to be buried in her hair, but I didn't want to scare her or for her to think I'd hold her down there as she ran out of air too.

I parted my lips at her insistence, intent on taking over the kiss when she pushed the air from her lungs into mine. With a tap against my chin, my slow brain processed what she was doing. I couldn't waste the gift she'd given. My eyes opened, and I closed my mouth, holding in the precious oxygen. She pushed away from the open doorway.

She'd bought me time by sharing her air until help arrived. I could only assume she'd left to get someone. I looked up but didn't see her ascending to the surface. *Where the hell had she gone?* My mind had latched onto her rather than my predicament. She looked younger than me. *Had to be seventeen? Hopefully eighteen? God, I hope she made it out.*

When she reappeared, my brows furrowed. I waved my hand to the surface. She shook her head. Once more, she grabbed the back of my neck and fitted her lips over mine. I didn't waste time with confusion. She fed me oxygen. It tasted flat, stale, but my straining lungs greedily accepted it.

I leaned as far as I could and glimpsed her feet by the front tire. *That's where she was getting the air? Smart.*

As I waited for her to return, my mind spun. *Is she the one who'd hit my car? Had to be. Why else is she here, helping me so soon after I'd gone over the bridge?*

When she returned, I looked her over. There wasn't a scratch on her. She was beautiful, ethereal. I committed everything I could to memory in the dim glow of my interior lights.

A faint sound echoed through the water. Her hands

gripped the side of my face, and she forced more air into my mouth, more than last time. Unable to stop myself, I lifted my hands and cupped her face. Her touch left me. There was a tug on the strap holding me in place. The belt gave away, then she broke the seal she had over my lips. She glanced up, and her delicate features hardened. Twisting, she pushed off the side of the door and swam away in the direction from which she'd come.

Light shone in a beam through the water as I worked free of the severed belt. *Why had she fled?* I glanced up. Red and blue lights danced over the water in addition to the floodlights in each of the two rescuers' grips. I shoved away from the car and swam upward.

One thing I knew was that the girl had gone, and there had to be a reason for it. The only thing that mattered was that she'd saved me. I owed her my life.

Nadia

My HEAD BROKE the water's surface as I stepped onto the rocky bank. Flashing lights drew anyone within range to the side of the bridge where Cade's car had busted through and then fallen into the water.

Beneath the water, noise had been muted. Out of the river, sound returned. It was New York, after all, the city that never slept.

He'd been my mark, one I'd let myself get involved with— even if from afar—outside the mission. My fingers pressed against my swollen lips and considered the reaction I'd had to touching him under the water. It'd been to keep him alive, nothing more. But it was so much more, and I was shocked. He wasn't for me, if anyone was. I had a job to do, and there was no time for foolish thoughts.

Relief coursed through me in a steady stream, mixed with anxiety over the next part of my mission. Darting my gaze around, I emerged from the river once I caught sight of the icy blonde, Hannah. She was a defector-flipped-sleeper-agent who scared me to death but had also offered salvation. With her help, I had a chance to escape.

I slogged through rock and mud until I stood before the small grouping of trees where she waited. Just out of view, I joined her within the cover. My teeth chattered, and she handed me a blanket. After I wrapped it around myself, I willed the physical discomfort away. Her icy gaze narrowed. I knew what she was thinking. I was better than that—I shouldn't let the temperature get to me. I had been trained by Russian operatives, and I could withstand much more than a short duration in chilly water.

Squaring my shoulders, I met her gaze with determination. I let her see the steel inside of me. I could do it. No emotion flashed across her face, and I schooled mine to match.

"Did you get them?" she asked.

At her clipped, no-nonsense question, I notched my chin. "Did you stop them?"

If I hadn't been staring so hard, I would have missed the minuscule tilt of her lips. I'd amused her. That was better than anger. She awarded me with a brisk nod. All the fight left me. The two people I'd lived with for the past twelve years were no longer my problem.

"And the girl?" I asked.

"She's safe."

I dug in my pocket and tugged the keys loose that I'd swiped from Cade's car. I dangled them between us. Her fingers closed around them before she dropped them into the purse at her side. "Let's go."

A burst of hope shot through me. *This is it.* For my assistance, she would take me away from there. I couldn't help myself—I took one last glance toward the bridge. Then I turned, shedding the life I'd had and the obsession I'd developed for the person I was supposed to kill.

To continue reading Moonlit Mirage CLICK HERE.

https://amymckinleyauthor.com/moonlit-destination-series/

ACKNOWLEDGMENTS

This is one of my favorite stories. Words whispered and haunting scenes lured me to walk hand in hand with Gianna and Sergio, and of course, Giovanni and Sophia. When they beckon, the soft strains of violins permeate the air, and their story unfolds in spell-like wonder. My hope as you read this book is that you, too, are transported to another world.

There are so many people that I want to thank that have encouraged me along the way, especially to my family, for their support and unwavering belief.

Taylor Anhalt is always there to bounce ideas, write together while we push ourselves to meet tight deadlines, and help with editing. We are getting closer to being able to write at Panera!

Huge thanks to my amazing critique team—I don't know what I would do without you! Kristin Kisska, with your extensive travel knowledge and suspense-inclined mind, has been invaluable and greatly appreciated. Emily Albright, thank you for the wealth of kindness and support, jumping in at a moment's notice, and for always being there to bounce ideas. To Candace Irving while we hash things out over the phone, compare notes, and your invaluable attention to structure. These women are incredibly talented authors and true rockstars, and I'm very fortunate to have them as friends and colleagues.

To Kate Birdsall, who I've had the privilege of working with for the past few years—you make my books shine!

To Colleen Noyes, the owner of Itsy Bitsy Book Bits, and her unfailing encouragement, support, and friendship. I couldn't imagine having a book release without having an IBBB tour; it's a staple in my marketing plan. Colleen's staff and readers are wonderful and dedicated and so very appreciated.

Thank you to Danielle Sanchez, owner of Wildfire Marketing Solutions, for all the encouragement and strategizing.

T.E. Black Designs, who designed the cover. We've done so many covers together over the years, and each one exceeds my expectations.

Some days are more difficult than others to get the work done, and as a sculptor, Maryellen Newton knows firsthand how the process goes. Thank you for cracking that whip, telling me to keep my butt in the chair, and write the story. I don't know what I would do without our weekly coffee time!

And a huge thank you to all the bloggers and readers who have encouraged and helped me along the way and who continue to make my dream a reality.

Thank you.

If you enjoyed reading MOONLIT KISS as much as I did writing it, I hope you'll consider leaving a review.

 Amy McKinley is the *USA Today* Bestselling Author of the romantic suspense thriller Gray Ghost Novels, Deadly Isles Special Ops, Covert Recruits, Moonlit Destination Series, Mafia Elite, the Five Fates paranormal romance books, and several standalone titles. Her edge-of-your-seat books are filled with surprising twists and just the right amount of heat and danger. She lives in Illinois with her husband, two daughters, two sons, and three mischievous cats.

You can find her at:
www.AmyMcKinley.com

Subscribe to Amy's newsletter for cover reveals, book announcements, and giveaways: http://eepurl.com/dEBqJn

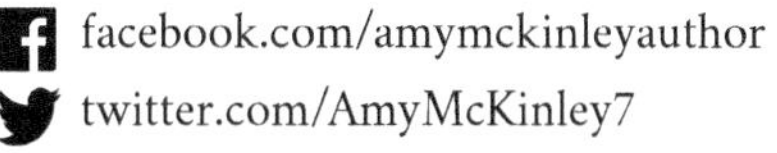

facebook.com/amymckinleyauthor
twitter.com/AmyMcKinley7
instagram.com/amymckinleyauthor

Moonlit Destination Series

Moonlit Whisper

Moonlit Kiss

Moonlit Mirage

Mafia Elite (coming soon)

No Way Out

Blood Oath

Born in Darkness

Five Fates Series

Hidden

Taken